"Get in the cabin," Lance yelled. "I'll cover you."

"We'll cover each other."

He frowned but there was no time to argue. They both fired their pistols toward the trees as they raced up the steps and charged into the house. This time she was the one who slammed the door shut and flipped the lock. Lance pulled her to the floor beneath the front windows. He covered her body with his as bullets slammed into the front door.

Keira shoved at him, her lungs straining for air beneath his tight hold even as her sore ribs screamed in pain. "You know I'm a cop, right?" She forced the words out, then dragged in another painful breath. "I can defend myself. Get off me."

"I'm not going to cower while a woman takes a bullet for me."

She shoved at him, cursing.

He laughed. "Maybe you should have been a sailor. Those are some salty words coming out of that pretty mouth."

"You think this is funny? People are trying to kill us."

"Not the first time. Won't be the last."

SMOKY MOUNTAINS MYSTERY

LENA DIAZ

INTRIGUE

Harlequin® INTRIGUE™

Recycling programs for this product may not exist in your area.

ISBN-13: 978-1-335-45697-7

Smoky Mountains Mystery

Copyright © 2024 by Lena Diaz

All rights reserved. No part of this book may be used or reproduced in any manner whatsoever without written permission.

Without limiting the author's and publisher's exclusive rights, any unauthorized use of this publication to train generative artificial intelligence (AI) technologies is expressly prohibited.

This is a work of fiction. Names, characters, places and incidents are either the product of the author's imagination or are used fictitiously. Any resemblance to actual persons, living or dead, businesses, companies, events or locales is entirely coincidental.

For questions and comments about the quality of this book, please contact us at CustomerService@Harlequin.com.

TM and ® are trademarks of Harlequin Enterprises ULC.

Harlequin Enterprises ULC
22 Adelaide St. West, 41st Floor
Toronto, Ontario M5H 4E3, Canada
www.Harlequin.com

Printed in Lithuania

MIX
Paper | Supporting responsible forestry
FSC® C021394

Lena Diaz was born in Kentucky and has also lived in California, Louisiana and Florida, where she now resides with her husband and two children. Before becoming a romantic suspense author, she was a computer programmer. A Romance Writers of America Golden Heart® Award finalist, she has also won the prestigious Daphne du Maurier Award for Excellence in Mystery/Suspense. To get the latest news about Lena, please visit her website, lenadiaz.com.

Books by Lena Diaz

Harlequin Intrigue

A Tennessee Cold Case Story

Murder on Prescott Mountain
Serial Slayer Cold Case
Shrouded in the Smokies
The Secret She Keeps
Smoky Mountains Graveyard
Smoky Mountains Mystery

The Justice Seekers

Cowboy Under Fire
Agent Under Siege
Killer Conspiracy
Deadly Double-Cross

Visit the Author Profile page at Harlequin.com.

CAST OF CHARACTERS

Lance Cabrera—A cold case investigator employed by a private firm called Unfinished Business. Lance's secret past comes back to haunt him, putting everyone he cares about in danger.

Keira Sloane—Frustrated at her small-town police department not giving her a chance to become a detective, she secretly takes on a case they let go cold. The case heats up when she tracks the evidence to Lance Cabrera.

Ileana Sanchez—Lance hasn't seen Ileana, his old girlfriend, in years. Suddenly she's back on the scene, causing tension and raising all kinds of questions about what really happened back when they were a couple.

Ian Murphy—He was Lance's boss years earlier, and his death changed the course of Lance's life, along with his old investigative team. Was Murphy behind those deaths, or simply a victim?

Rick Cameron—Once a good friend of Lance's, Rick is murdered in a cheap motel. When the clues point to Lance, Keira is determined to solve this cold case and find out whether Lance is a killer.

Levi Alexander—Levi was killed three months before Rick, and the only link that seems to tie these two deaths together is that they used to work with Lance.

Chapter One

Keira Sloane two-handed her service weapon, elbows bent, pistol pointing up toward the ceiling as she flattened her back against the wall outside the motel room. The dim lights from the dark parking lot one story below glinted off the rusty railing across from her. Chuck Breamer, one of two fellow officers with her, mirrored her stance on the other side of the door. In front of him, Gabe Wilson held his gun pointed down. He glanced at Chuck, then Keira. After receiving their nods, he rapped loudly on the door again before jerking back to avoid potential gunfire.

"Maple Falls Police. Last chance. Open the door." As with the first knock, there was no response.

Gabe held up three fingers, silently counting down. *Three, two, one.* He delivered a vicious kick to the doorknob. The frame splintered. The ruined door flew open and crashed against the wall, making the large window beside the door rattle.

All three ran inside, sweeping their guns back and forth.

The metallic smell of blood struck Keira immediately. A wounded or dead man lay on the bed closest to the window. She quickly checked behind the chair in the corner for any hidden suspects while her fellow officers checked under both beds.

"Main room clear," she announced.

Chuck jogged to the doorway on the back left. Gabe checked the one on the back right.

"Bathroom's clear," Chuck said.

"Closet clear," Gabe echoed. "No one else is here." He motioned toward an indentation in the cheap floral comforter covering the empty bed where it appeared that someone had sat at one time. "At least, not anymore."

Keira holstered her pistol and rushed to the side of the victim's bed, grimacing in sympathy at the extent of his injuries. Dressed only in navy blue boxers, the approximately thirty-year-old Black man was mottled with bruises and cuts on all of his extremities, with most of the damage to his chest.

Beneath him, the formerly white sheet was turning red. Blood dripped down, adding to a growing wet tangle of carpet. When she pressed her fingers against the side of his neck, to her surprise it was warm. There was a weak, thready pulse.

"He's alive. Get a bus out here."

Chuck radioed for an ambulance.

Keira grabbed the edge of the comforter and used it to apply pressure to what appeared to be bullet entrance wounds on his chest. Someone had beaten and tortured this man before shooting him. He'd lost so much blood it was a miracle that he was still alive, even more of a miracle if he made it to the hospital.

A hand grabbed her wrist, making her jump. She was shocked that it was the man on the bed. He stared up at her with pain-glazed dark brown eyes, his hand clutching hers. But whatever strength he had immediately drained away. His hand fell back to the mattress.

"Hold on," she told him. "Don't go into the light, buddy. Help's on the way."

His face turned ashen as his lips moved. But she couldn't make out what he said.

She leaned close. "Say it again," she encouraged him.

"L... Lance," the faint whisper sounded.

"Lance," she echoed. "Hang on, Lance. I'm Keira. I'm a cop. We're here to help you and—"

"Move." Chuck roughly pushed her out of the way.

"He's bleeding," she said. "His chest—"

"I've got it." His prior experience as an EMT kicked in as he maintained pressure on the victim's chest with one hand and checked his airway with the other.

Keira watched with a growing feeling of helplessness as Chuck assessed the victim. She wanted to help. But of the three of them, Chuck had the best chance of keeping him alive until the ambulance arrived.

She turned to check on Gabe and saw him reaching for the top drawer of the cheap particle-board dresser opposite the two beds.

"We need a warrant," she reminded him. "Exigent circumstances are over." Even though the motel manager was the one who'd called 911, he hadn't formally given them permission to search once they'd responded to the report of "shots fired."

Gabe shrugged and dropped his hand. "The lieutenant's on his way. Knowing him, he'll already have the warrant anyway."

She smiled at his statement. They both knew no one, not even their scarily efficient supervisor, Owen Jackson, could have gotten a warrant that fast.

Chuck straightened and stepped back from the bed. "He's gone. On top of being treated like a punching bag and sliced with a knife, he was shot at least three times. There's nothing anyone could have done to save this guy."

Keira blew out a shaky breath. Her wrist tingled as if the man were still holding it. He'd wanted her help. But she hadn't been able to do anything to change his fate. "Lance. His name is Lance."

Chuck frowned. "You know this guy?"

"No. He whispered it. Lance. Might have been Vance or Vince. But I think it was Lance."

"Did he say it was *his* name? Maybe it was the killer's name."

She winced. "I hope not. I called him Lance."

"We'll know soon enough, once we get a warrant to search for his wallet. Assuming it wasn't stolen." He started typing a text, no doubt updating their boss on the current status.

She glanced around the small room. Even the blood spatter on the wall behind the victim didn't mask the years of grime. But, aside from the twisted, bloody covers on the bed, everything else was neat and orderly. The dresser and nightstand drawers were closed. No belongings had been dumped onto the floor and rifled through. The second bed was made with the pillows and comforter in place.

"The room doesn't look tossed," she said. "His business suit's lying over there on that chair, as if he'd planned on wearing it tomorrow. It's rumpled, so the killer may have checked the pockets. But if this was a robbery, you'd think they'd take the suit. It's not cheap. Could fetch a few hundred at a consignment shop."

Gabe joined them. "I doubt a robber in this part of

town would recognize the value of a suit or want to bother with it. But they'd definitely have taken the fancy Mercedes out front that the manager said belongs to this guy. Why would a man who can afford a car like that stay in a nasty, cheap motel?"

Keira glanced at the man on the bed, wishing he could answer those questions, that he'd wake up in the morning and call his family, his friends. Tell them who'd attacked him and why. "Maybe he was hiding out from someone who'd never expect him to stay in a place like this." She shrugged. "That's one of many things we'll have to figure out."

Gabe gave her a doubtful look. "What makes you think Owen is finally going to let you play detective?"

She stiffened. "I can play whodunit as well as anyone else. I'm ready."

He held his hands up in a placating gesture. "No argument here. It's the LT you have to convince."

Chuck slid his cell phone back in his pocket. "We need to identify potential witnesses before they scatter like ants in a thunderstorm. Gabe, you take the rooms to the right. I'll go left. Names and addresses, verified with ID. We can't force them to hang around. But at least we can follow up with them once we have more manpower."

"Or woman power," Keira said. "I'll help."

Chuck frowned. "You're on guard duty. If the EMTs get here before we're back, try to keep them from destroying evidence. Once they verify our victim is DOA, get them out of our crime scene."

Gabe sent her an apologetic glance as he closed the door behind him and Chuck.

Chapter Two

Keira swore. How was she ever going to advance in the tiny town of Maple Falls, Tennessee, if her fellow officers kept coddling her and never gave her a chance? She knew exactly why they'd told her to wait here for the EMTs. In spite of them all being sworn law enforcement officers, her male counterparts couldn't set aside their Southern manners to treat a woman like one of the guys.

Even though she had a uniform on, they saw the woman first, the cop second. They didn't want her doing knock-and-talks and putting herself at risk in this part of town. Three years. She'd been working with them for three years, and she was still the lowest one on the food chain, the last to be given real opportunities to make a difference.

A quick glance at the shooting victim had guilt riding her hard. Here she was worrying about her career, her future. At least she *had* a future. This man, who was in his prime, had no future. His life had ended in violence and pain. What mattered right now was getting justice for him.

She edged closer to the bed, careful to avoid the bloodiest section of the carpet. He was a handsome man, with closely shaved black hair, his skin a medium brown color. The absence of a gold band on his ring finger meant he likely wasn't married. But he still might have a child, or children, perhaps an ex-wife or girlfriend. If he had siblings or parents still alive, people who loved him, they'd be devastated by his loss.

This was why she wanted to become a detective.

It was too depressing being bombarded on a daily basis by the awful things that human beings did to each other without some ray of hope or happiness. She craved the good parts of the job. She wanted to be the one to give a family the answers they desperately needed, the why and the who behind whatever had happened to their loved one. That would be the ultimate reward. Putting a name with the face of tonight's victim was the first step toward getting him, and his family, justice.

She glanced at the closed door. Would it really hurt to look for his wallet? Just to check his driver's license so she'd be sure about his name? If she was careful, if she wore gloves, she wouldn't destroy potential evidence or muck it up with her own DNA and fingerprints. She could already hear faint, distant sirens. The ambulance would be here soon, a few minutes out at most. If she was going to cross a line and not get caught, she had to do it now.

Always prepared, she had a pair of latex gloves in her pocket. She quickly pulled them on and went on the hunt for a wallet. It wasn't in the pockets of the suit jacket or in the dresser drawer. Instead, it was neatly sitting in the top drawer of the vanity in the bathroom, along with a ring of keys and his car's key fob.

Her heart seemed to squeeze in her chest when she flipped open the wallet and saw a photograph in a plastic sleeve. A little girl, probably no more than two, was in his arms, pressing a kiss against his cheek. He'd been a father after all. Or maybe an uncle or family friend. He was clearly loved and would be missed. She swallowed against the tightness in her throat and pulled his driver's license out. When she saw his name, her stomach sank. Rick. His name was Rick Cameron. The name he'd given her wasn't his.

Forgive me, Rick. I'm so sorry that I called you Lance, especially if he's the killer.

The victim's address was in Baton Rouge, Louisiana. She snapped a quick picture with her cell phone camera. Then she risked a precious few more seconds to check the rest of the wallet.

There were more pictures, a couple of credit cards and two one-hundred dollar bills. This definitely hadn't been a robbery. She started to set the wallet back in the drawer when a flash of white stopped her. Tucked into a credit card sleeve was a small piece of paper. She took it out and carefully unfolded it. There were two words written in a neat cursive script.

unfinished business

Voices sounded in the hallway outside the room. Keira quickly snapped a picture, then hurriedly refolded the note and put everything back the way she'd found it.

The squeak of the exterior door told her that someone had just entered the motel room.

"Keira? You in here?"

Chuck. Dang it. "In the bathroom. Give me a sec." She flushed the toilet and then flipped on the faucet as if she were washing her hands and hurriedly shoved her gloves into her pocket. When she stepped out, Chuck was standing with his hands on his hips while Gabe directed the EMTs toward the bed with the victim.

"You couldn't wait and use the bathroom in the motel office?" Chuck's voice was frigid.

Her face flushed warm as the EMTs glanced curiously at her. She knew the rules, knew not to disturb the scene. Heck, she'd warned Gabe not to open a drawer earlier. But she'd rather Chuck think she'd forgotten or had gotten sloppy than to tell him the truth—that she'd rummaged through the dead man's belongings knowing full well she shouldn't have.

"Sorry. It hit me all of a sudden." She gave him a pained smile as she strode toward him. "How did you two finish your knock-and-talks so fast?"

Gabe joined them near the dresser, giving the EMTs space to confirm the victim was beyond help. "Most of the rooms were empty, curtains open, beds made. We could tell there wasn't anyone inside refusing to come to the door. Lots of vacancies in this place." He wrinkled his nose as he glanced around. "Go figure, huh?"

"Not exactly the Ritz."

Gabe smiled.

Chuck didn't. He stared at her, his disapproval thick in the air, before turning to respond to a question from one of the EMTs.

Gabe gave her a sympathetic look before joining Chuck.

Keira blew out a frustrated breath. *Stupid.* She should have waited for the official investigation to find out the victim's name. No doubt she'd hurt her chances to be included on the case. If it had only been Gabe who'd caught her, he'd have kept it quiet. But by-the-book Chuck Breamer would no doubt tell their supervisor what she'd done at the first opportunity.

Sure enough, when the LT arrived, Chuck's summary

of everything the three of them had done included her trip to the bathroom. Their boss's words fell on her like a death knell as he barked his orders.

"Wilson, secure the crime scene until we can borrow a CSI tech from the DeKalb County Sheriff's Office to assist out here. Breamer, interview the motel manager. Get their surveillance video, assuming the cameras outside even work. Sloane—" his flinty gaze zeroed in on her "—let's see if you can manage to return to the station and write up your report without touching anything on the way out."

Gabe winced. Chuck didn't even look her way as he headed outside, presumably to speak to the manager.

Keira straightened her shoulders and took the walk of shame past her supervisor without comment.

By the time Keira finished her report, she wanted to kick herself for screwing up.

Gabe, upon his return to the station, had reluctantly admitted that Owen had said he'd planned on letting her help on the investigation—until he'd heard about what she'd done. Now she'd likely have to spend several more months trying to earn another chance.

Murders rarely happened in Maple Falls. So even if she was given a chance, it probably wouldn't be on a case this important. It would likely be on a stolen property investigation or a domestic violence situation that she could wrap up in less than a day. Her original plan in leaving Nashville PD to join a small police department because there'd be less competition definitely wasn't going the way she'd expected. She was beginning to think it was the worst mistake she'd ever made.

Gabe, her only true friend around here, kept sending

her looks of pity from across the squad room. Unable to take it anymore, she locked up her desk and left the station ten minutes early. If that was enough for Owen to write her up, so be it. At this point, she was too depressed to even care.

Later at home, in a calmer frame of mind, she reluctantly admitted that Owen wasn't petty enough to worry about ten minutes unless it was habitual. She was almost never late and rarely left early. But she had no doubt she'd still be written up for not following policy at a crime scene. And he was right to do it. She hadn't followed the rules. In fact, she'd broken them far worse than anyone knew.

She thumbed through the pictures on her cell phone that she'd taken in the motel bathroom. Technically, she should log them into evidence and then erase them from her personal device. The fact that she had no intention of doing either of those things could mean that her boss was right in thinking that she wasn't cut out to be a detective.

Forget that. She'd make a great detective. The only reason she occasionally broke the rules was because it was the only way to be let in on the action.

She studied Rick Cameron's driver's license photograph and the picture of his note. *Unfinished business* was cop slang for a cold case. But that didn't make sense in this context, especially since there wasn't anything in Rick Cameron's wallet to suggest he was a police officer working a case. Then again, if he was truly undercover, she wouldn't expect him to carry official police ID.

But that theory seemed weak. What kind of cold case would lead a detective from Louisiana to DeKalb County and the tiny Middle Tennessee town of Maple Falls? With a population just over two thousand, it wasn't exactly a sprawling metropolis where criminals fled to from big cities around the country to escape justice. Rick Cameron had to be passing through. To where? There was only one way to find out. She'd conduct her own investigation. And she'd do whatever it took to solve it, get justice for Rick and his loved ones, and prove herself.

When she presented her findings to the lieutenant, he'd be forced to recognize her as worthy enough to be allowed to work as a detective when warranted. Their ten-person police force didn't have any full-time detectives. Maple Falls was too small to justify that. And only a select few were allowed to act as detective when needed—like Chuck.

She grabbed her laptop computer from the end table and opened up an internet search.

THREE WEEKS LATER, Keira had little to show for her secret investigation into the motel murder. But neither did anyone else. As she sat at her desk in the squad room snooping through the latest printed copies she'd made from the official case files, her stomach sank at the lack of progress.

The name Lance had led nowhere. There weren't any local thugs on their radar with Lance as either their first or last name. A brief bio stated that the victim worked in the computer tech industry, remotely from home. He was a contract programmer currently in between contracts. That explained why an employer hadn't reported him missing.

He lived alone. No one in his neighborhood had ever noticed any family members visiting him, in spite of those pictures in his wallet. They hadn't noticed friends visiting either. Keira had no idea who the little girl was in the photo in Rick's wallet. All she could figure was that it was a friend's child and that she'd read far too much into it. After all, if he was close to that friend, or that little girl was part of his life, wouldn't someone in that circle have contacted the police by now, asking where he was? Baton Rouge law enforcement was supposed to let Maple Falls know if someone inquired about him. So far, that hadn't happened. With no friends, family or loved ones to advocate for him, no one was pushing the Maple Falls Police to keep digging and figure out who'd killed Rick Cameron.

None of the potential eyewitnesses at the motel had offered much of value either. The last person to make any notes in the case file was Chuck. And that had been four days ago. The case was already cold. Soon it would go into a deep freeze.

Gabe stopped by her desk and balanced a hip on the corner. "Two weeks off starting tomorrow, huh? Bet you're looking forward to it. Where you going?"

She shuffled the papers on her desk, mainly to hide her copies of reports from the Cameron case. "Probably what I do every vacation. Sit at home and watch TV, take naps. Lots of naps."

He clucked his tongue. "That's a waste, especially for a cute little brunette like you. Go do something fun. Pick up a guy. Trust me. For someone with your looks, it would be easy." At her eye roll, he laughed. "Okay, okay. Maybe you should pay a visit back home. Nashville, right? You must have some family or friends back there who'd love to see you."

Her only response was to stare at him. Although they were friends, she refused to discuss her family with him or anyone. The situation was…complicated. Going to see them during her two weeks off definitely wasn't on her itinerary.

When he gave up with his less than subtle interrogation, he wandered off to someone else's desk. Keira stuffed the papers she'd hidden into her purse and headed out. Her suitcase was already in her car. Let the so-called vacation begin.

Ten minutes later, she was at the town cemetery standing at the back corner where those without money or with no one to claim their bodies were buried. Pauper's graves. That felt so wrong for Rick Cameron.

His suit was expensive. The car he'd driven to the motel was a late-model Mercedes. He could afford a better burial. But he'd left no will, and his estate was tied up in the courts. For now, at least, he was here.

Keira placed the white silk roses she'd purchased earlier in the little vase beside the grave marker. It was a small slab of marble with only his name and dates. Normally a grave the city dug would only have a cheap metal marker with numbers on it. But Keira had scrabbled together enough money to buy the little marble headstone and vase. The man had used his last bit of strength to clutch her arm and whisper his dying word. How could she not give him a headstone after that?

Unfinished business. That note from his wallet was what had set her on her current path. It had cemented where she was going during her time off. After performing hundreds of internet searches on that phrase over the past few weeks, resulting in millions of useless hits, this morning she'd had better luck. She'd keyed in a ridiculously long string of additional search terms and the top result that popped up had her staring at the screen for a long time.

Unfinished Business, with both words capitalized, was the name of a private company in Gatlinburg, Tennessee, about four hours from Maple Falls. The purpose of the company? They investigated cold cases for law enforcement throughout the East Tennessee region. Since Maple Falls was in Middle Tennessee, they didn't officially support her county, which was why she'd never heard of them before. But here was the kicker. One of the investigators listed on their website had a name she'd rarely heard, until a few weeks ago.

Lance.

The odds were astronomical against UB's Lance Cabrera being the Lance that the victim had whispered with his final breath. Or even that UB was the same unfinished business listed on the note, especially since Rick hadn't capitalized either word. But the two things together seemed like a sign, a good omen that going there might help. Somehow.

Best scenario, UB and this Lance guy might actually know Rick Cameron and could lead to a resolution of the case. Worst scenario, they knew nothing about the victim. But as cold-case professionals they might give her some expert advice on how to proceed. Either way, it was a win.

She touched a hand to the cold marble. "Chances are a million to one against this being a real lead, Mr. Cameron. Or that this Lance guy I've found is *your* Lance. But it's all I have. Hopefully something will come out of this that will put your killer or killers in prison. I'm off to Gatlinburg to take care of your *unfinished business.*"

A crunching sound had her whirling around. No one was there. The cemetery was empty. Her silver Camry was about fifty yards away, the only vehicle in the parking lot. She scanned the tree line behind the chain-link fence. Nothing. It was probably just the light breeze blowing through the trees, making some branches click together. Or an animal rooting around in the woods, stepping on dried leaves that were everywhere, with it being the middle of autumn. But that didn't stop the unease that settled in her gut. After one last scan, she hurried toward her car, pistol out and at the ready.

Chapter Three

Lance Cabrera had always known his days were numbered. That the past would catch up to him sooner or later. But he'd really been hoping for later. Much later.

He kept his expression bland as the pretty young officer from Maple Falls told her story to him and his fellow cold-case investigators. She sat across the table from him in one of the glass-walled conference rooms of Unfinished Business, perched near the top of Prescott Mountain overlooking Gatlinburg, Tennessee, far below.

In the past, someone bringing UB a case who wasn't from the Tennessee Bureau of Investigation or an East Tennessee law enforcement agency wouldn't have gotten past the front door. But that rule had been eased after one of their own was abducted because they'd turned away the wrong person.

Now, when they could spare a few moments, they'd at least listen to people lobbying for their help outside of their contracted area. That help usually took the form of advice or referrals to other agencies. But their main goal was to determine whether the person was a potential threat.

This petite, brown-eyed, dark-haired wannabe detective—Keira Sloane—probably didn't concern the other UB investigators in the room. But in the twenty minutes that she'd been speaking and answering questions, he'd recognized the enormous threat she offered not only to him but to everyone in this room—including herself.

She tapped the pile of pictures she'd set on top of the table—crime scene photos she'd admittedly copied from the official case file. She was painfully honest, not even attempting to pretend that she wasn't supposed to be working on this case.

"There's one more thing," she said.

Her dark gaze locked with his. He could almost feel the nails pounding into his coffin as he waited for her next words.

"I told you the note in the victim's wallet said 'unfinished business,' which led me here. But he also *said* something to me right before he died."

Grayson Prescott, the genius businessman billionaire and former Army Ranger who'd created UB, leaned forward at the head of the long conference room table. "Don't keep us in suspense, Officer Sloane. What did Mr. Cameron tell you?"

"It was one word, a name. With his dying breath, he whispered, 'Lance.'"

Lance couldn't help wincing, thinking of Rick whispering his name as he lay dying in a motel room. At least he hadn't died alone. Lance would be forever grateful that Officer Sloane's kind face was the last one Rick saw, not the face of his killer.

"Hell of a coincidence," Ryland Beck, their lead investigator, said.

"It is," Lance agreed, careful to keep his grief from his voice, his expression. He had to play this carefully. A lot was on the line. "But I wouldn't call it compelling. There's no obvious connection between the note and what

he said. The words *unfinished business* weren't capitalized like they would be if it was our company's name. It
was likely just a reminder that this Cameron guy needed
to take care of something."

"That's one theory," Sloane allowed. "Another is that
he knew someone was after him, so he wrote that note
in lowercase letters on purpose to throw them off if they
found it."

"Why even have the note if he was worried that someone might find it?"

"I've asked myself that same question. The only thing
that rings true to me is that he specifically hoped someone
would find the note if something happened to him. To the
killer, it meant nothing. But to law enforcement, well, we
dig. We don't stop until we make sense of the evidence.
That phrase is a clue, a breadcrumb left by a murdered
man who whispered your name as a second breadcrumb.
He anticipated that an investigator would follow that trail
here. The question is, Why? And what does it have to do
with you, Mr. Cabrera?"

He chuckled as if amused. "There's no way he could
have known there'd be someone with him when he died
and that he'd be able to give them a name."

"That occurred to me as well."

"And?"

She shrugged. "If I had everything figured out, I
wouldn't be here asking for help."

"Fair enough. How certain are you that he said 'Lance'?
Could it have been Vance? Vince? Something else? You
said he bled out. I doubt his mind was firing on all cyl-
inders. He probably wasn't even aware of what he said.
It was random."

Her face reddened slightly, whether from embarrassment or anger, he wasn't sure. "He was lucid, his eyes clear as he looked at me. Could I have heard him wrong? Possibly. But I truly believe he said Lance."

"You truly believe?" he scoffed, trying to make light of her rather impressive conclusions that were likely spot on. "Let's assume you're correct. Why link that name to his murder? Maybe it was the name of a family member or friend, and he wanted them to know he was thinking about them at the end."

"My team explored those possibilities. He has no family that we've been able to discover. No friends that we know of. The name Lance had to hold some kind of significance for him to use his last breath to give me that information."

Lance's fists were clenched so hard beneath the table that his hands were going numb. He forced himself to relax his grip.

"If he truly said 'Lance,' and was lucid, how does that help you? It's not a common name. But it's not exactly rare either. It could be someone's first name or their last name. I'm sure if you run an internet search, you'll come up with thousands of hits in Tennessee alone. Did you? Run a search?"

Her eyes narrowed. She didn't appreciate him challenging her investigative skills and wasn't doing well at hiding her resentment. Good. Her defensiveness would help cast doubt on her conclusions.

She crossed her arms over her ample chest, making her appear even more defensive. "I searched our local law enforcement databases, as well as some national ones for known criminals with that name. Nothing of significance came up for our area. And you're correct that my internet searches yielded a large number of hits. But the name

Lance linked to a company called Unfinished Business? That combination only came up once and led me to you."

A ripple of unease seemed to eddy through the room. Lance sighed heavily and sat back. "I don't buy that for a second. You'd have gotten thousands of hits on that phrase, tens of thousands. There's no way you hunted all of those down and then determined only one hit was connected to the name Lance in any way. You're reaching. I totally get that. I've been there, many times. But jumping from point A to point Z without anything in between isn't how you find the *right* answers. Please tell me you have something else—facts, some actual evidence—for you to have come all this way and taken up our valuable time with your theories."

An elbow jabbed his ribs.

Frowning at Faith sitting to his left, he rubbed his side. "What was that for?"

"Manners," she said. "Remember those? Our team doesn't belittle people who come to us for assistance."

He glanced around the table. Pretty much everyone was looking at him with disapproval. He felt a flush creeping up his neck. Belittling someone, as Faith had put it, wasn't how he typically treated anyone, especially a woman. Apparently he was coming across as a bully and Sloane the sympathetic victim.

If the stakes weren't so high, he'd apologize profusely and shut up. And he'd do everything he could to make it up to Sloane for how he'd been acting. But the stakes *were* high, and this wasn't just about him. If he couldn't discredit Sloane's theories, both her and anyone in this room who might decide to assist her with the case was in jeopardy.

"All right, all right." He held up his hands in a placating gesture. "I might have been overzealous in playing the devil's advocate, looking for holes in your conclusions. It wasn't my intention to be offensive, to come across as a—"

"Jerk?" Faith offered.

Several of those around the table laughed.

Officer Sloane's brows rose, apparently unsure whether they were teasing or not.

Lance waited for the laughter to die down. Time for a more direct approach, to go for the jugular.

"I won't argue that particular conclusion," he allowed. "I've behaved badly. And although I don't excuse how I've acted, I hope everyone can at least understand it. After all, it's not every day that someone comes to my place of employment and essentially accuses me of being involved in a murder. That is why you're here, isn't it, Officer Sloane? Because you think that I may have killed Mr. Cameron?"

She arched a brow in challenge. "Did you?"

Grayson rapped his knuckles on the table. "Enough." His hard tone cracked through the room. "Accusing one of my investigators of murder won't be tolerated."

Her eyes widened. "I...ah... I didn't mean to... I mean, I did, but I didn't—"

"Wait," Lance said, ready to play his trump card. "Now that I understand Officer Sloane's...intentions, I can easily put her concerns at rest by offering up an important fact to go along with her misplaced theories."

She stiffened, her expression wary. "What *fact*?"

"My alibi of course."

She blinked in surprise.

He motioned to Faith and her husband beside her, fellow investigator Asher. "Where was I on the night that Mr. Cameron was killed?"

Faith frowned. "I don't—"

"At the beginning of this meeting, Officer Sloane said the victim was killed on September 22. In the early evening. Isn't that correct, Officer?"

"Around eight thirty, yes."

"Oh," Faith said. "Of course." She gave Sloane a pained smile. "Lance definitely couldn't have been involved." She motioned to Asher. "My husband and I had a housewarming party for UB's investigators that night. We were celebrating buying our first home together as a married couple. And before you ask, no, there isn't any possibility that Lance could have left without someone realizing he was gone. Although UB has administrative staff, an IT department and a forensics lab, the actual investigative team is small, less than a dozen of us. We're all close, more like family than friends. His absence would have been noticed."

Grayson gave Lance a subtle nod of approval and relaxed back in his chair. He'd been at the party too and no doubt was relieved that this could be put to rest so easily.

"Faith took an obscene amount of pictures," Lance teased, chuckling when she tried to elbow him again. "I'm sure I'm in more than a few of them. The metadata on the camera cards can prove the date and time each photo was taken. You mentioned that Maple Falls is in DeKalb County. Can't say I've ever been there. But I know my geography. That county is a good three and a half hours from here."

"Four, actually." Sloane sounded defeated, as if she were finally accepting that she was wrong. "More if you hit traffic."

Lance smiled apologetically. "I'm truly sorry to have been so hard on you. But I hope you can see now that the two clues you've put so much credence in have nothing to do with me or this company. They probably have nothing to do with your case at all."

She nodded, looking defeated.

Lance regretted being the one who'd made her feel that way. But he was enormously grateful that they'd all managed to dodge a bullet.

She offered a sheepish smile to Lance and Grayson. "I'm sorry that things went sideways. Diplomacy and tact have never been my strong points. And now I really am back at square one. I'll have to reexamine the entire case file and figure out another starting point, the true reason for that note and for why Rick Cameron whispered the name Lance. Honestly, I'm at a loss."

Lance stared at her in dismay. "You're not dropping the investigation? Letting the detectives in Maple Falls handle the case?"

"Detectives?" She shook her head. "We don't have any, not really. There's no lab, no IT department like you have here. Mr. Cameron's murder was investigated by a couple of our officers who are deemed qualified to be detectives when needed. In an emergency type of situation, our chief will ask the county sheriff for assistance. But he hates to do that and hasn't with this case aside from using their crime scene techs to gather forensic evidence. At this point, it's as cold as a case can get, even though it's less than a month old. That's why I'm working it on my own time. My vacation ends in less than two weeks. If I haven't solved the case by then, it might never be solved. To that end, if someone here has any tips or suggestions, I sure would appreciate it."

Grayson motioned around the table. "Everyone here, except me, used to be a detective in law enforcement. I recruited Ryland to help me recruit the others to work in the private sector when I started this company. These investigators represent decades of experience solving crimes. And you already know their current specialty is cold cases. I'm sure they can offer you some pointers."

The look of desperate eagerness on Sloane's face as the team began offering tips shot a feeling of dread through Lance. All of his arguments had been for nothing. This determined police officer wasn't going to stop digging after all. But at least Grayson and the team lead, Ryland, hadn't offered to pull any of the investigators off their current cases to officially work with her. That might be the only good thing to come out of today's meeting. Him playing his alibi card had taken away the need for them to work the case to prove his innocence. As long as it stayed that way, his friends were safe. But Sloane might not be, not if she'd done something to attract the killer's attention.

That's what Lance needed to know, what exactly she'd done so far, in detail. Maybe it wasn't too late for her. As long as the killer didn't consider her to be a threat, she was safe. But for him, everything had changed. The past had reared its ugly head again. He couldn't ignore it without risking anyone associated with him becoming collateral damage. Finding Rick's killer, and keeping the lid on their shared past, was paramount.

While Sloane furiously typed notes on her computer tablet, Lance took the opportunity to briefly study each of his friends.

Grayson Prescott—their leader, a military hero who'd come home to a murdered wife and a missing daughter. Instead of buckling beneath his grief and ensuing frustration over a case that went cold for years, he'd formed Unfinished Business. After UB solved Grayson's cold case, he'd dedicated the company to helping other families dealing with similar situations.

Next to Grayson was Willow, his current wife, a former Gatlinburg detective who'd helped him solve his first wife's murder and find his missing daughter alive and well.

Ryland Beck, their team lead.

Trent. His full name was Adam Trent. But no one ever called him Adam. He'd gone through hell and back to save a woman who'd been on the run for years against unknown enemies determined to kill her.

He smiled at Callum Wright, who'd spent his life hating his last name because of all the jokes about him being Mr. Right. Callum had once despised lawyers. Now he was married to one.

Asher and Faith Whitfield. When they'd ended up together, the only people who were surprised were Asher and Faith.

A few members of the team weren't here. Rowan Knight, their liaison with the TBI. Other fellow investigators, Brice Galloway and Ivy Shaw.

Lance cared deeply about each and every one of them.

When he happened to glance at the end of the table again, he was dismayed to see Grayson intently watching him. There were questions in Grayson's eyes. No doubt he'd noticed Lance studying his fellow investigators and wondered why. Hoping to turn Grayson's attention, Lance pretended interest in what Ryland was currently discussing with Sloane.

To Lance's relief, a few moments later, Grayson stood, signaling the end of the meeting. "Best of luck with your investigation, Officer. I wish we could have done more."

She began sliding her photographs and computer tablet into her leather satchel. "Everyone's been exceedingly generous with their time and advice. I really appreciate it."

The team slowly filed out of the glass-walled conference room and down the stairs to the war room below. It was a large open area with lofty two-story high ceilings so that anyone in the conference rooms could look down and potentially signal to other investigators to join them. Or anyone below could see who was upstairs, including Grayson's office beside the largest conference room.

Lance waited for the others to leave so he could time his exit with their guest's. He held the door open. "Officer Sloane—"

She paused in the opening. "Call me Keira, please. I think after practically coming to blows, we should be on a first-name basis, don't you?"

He laughed, genuinely amused. "Keira. If any of us come up with more ideas for your investigation, where can we reach you? Are you staying in Gatlinburg for a while?"

Her eyes widened. "I appreciate you asking. Although I admit to being—"

"Surprised?"

She nodded.

"My apologies again. I really didn't mean to come across so rudely. Your visit, what you said, caught me off guard." Understatement of the decade. "But that's no excuse for the way I treated you. Forgive me?"

The smile she gifted him with completely transformed her. Where before she'd been pretty, now she was…stunning. In another lifetime, maybe they could have been friends. Or more. In addition to being incredibly attractive, she had qualities he greatly admired: honesty, integrity and a quick mind. Normally he'd appreciate her stubbornness and refusal to give up on an investigation too. But right now those qualities were extremely inconvenient.

"You're forgiven." She handed him a business card. "I'm booked in a chalet for a couple of days, up Skyline Road. It's a small A-frame hanging off the side of the mountain with a driveway sloping so steeply down toward the cabin that I refuse to use it." She shivered for effect.

"I think I know the place. People make bets about whether a tourist will slide down that driveway one day and barrel through the house and off the mountain." At her horrified look, he grinned. "I'm teasing."

She blinked. "Oh, well, I'm still not using the driveway. I park on the street out front."

"Four-wheel drive, I hope. It's not cold enough to snow yet, but sometimes you need that extra power to get up these mountains."

"My Camry's got all-wheel drive. So far, it's been great at hugging the curves and holding the roads. I think I'll be okay."

"I'm sure you will." He slid the business card into an inside pocket of his suit jacket.

She started to leave, then stopped. "If anyone needs to call me, be sure to use the personal cell number on that card. Not my office number. Because, well—"

"You're not there. And your coworkers don't know you're playing detective." At the light flush on her face, he smiled again. "Your secret's safe with us. Have a good day, Officer Sloane."

She gave him a grateful smile. "Keira."

"Keira."

As she headed down the stairs, Lance paused at the top landing to watch her. The two-story windows of the war room looked out at the parking lot. True to her word, she got into a silver late-model Camry. He couldn't see the license plate to take down and potentially track her. But he didn't need to.

He knew exactly where she was going.

A few moments later, he reached his desk and grabbed his laptop computer.

"Hey, Lance." Asher motioned to him from his desk two aisles over. "Can you take a look at this?"

"Sorry, buddy. I've got something I need to take care of." He headed toward the exit.

"Catch me later, all right?" Asher called out.

"Will do." The lie was bitter on his tongue, especially when he turned in the doorway for one last look at his team and noticed Grayson and Ryland watching from Grayson's second-floor office. Lance nodded, then turned away, knowing he'd never see them again. Because, contrary to what he'd just told Asher, he was never coming back.

Chapter Four

Keira looked up from her computer tablet, surprised to hear a knock on the cabin's door. She'd gotten back from Unfinished Business a few minutes ago and had only just now settled in front of the coffee table to review her notes from the meeting.

Although she wasn't expecting trouble, someone stopping at this remote rental cabin deep in the mountains had her grabbing her service pistol from an end table. When she looked through the security peephole in the front door, no one was there. Even more surprising was that a black SUV with dark-tinted windows was turning down her steep driveway.

When the SUV's door opened, a familiar broad-shouldered figure stepped out. She blinked in surprise. As he pulled his shades off and slid them into one of the pockets of his charcoal-gray suit jacket, she shook her head. What in the world was Lance Cabrera doing here? And good grief, was he this handsome, and tall, when she'd seen him earlier? She'd been so pumped with adrenaline and nervous energy when she'd presented her information to the room full of investigators that she hadn't really paid attention to how ruggedly good-looking he was.

She set her pistol on a decorative table against the wall before opening the door.

"Mr. Cabrera," she said as he climbed the steps of the front porch. "What happened? Did I leave my favorite pen at UB and you rushed over to return it?"

His deep blue eyes crinkled at the corners with amusement. "I didn't notice any wayward writing instruments in the conference room when I left."

"Then I confess to being confused about why you'd show up here. I couldn't have made a good impression by essentially accusing you of murder. So I'm guessing you're not here to ask me out on a date."

He grinned. "If I thought you'd be amenable, and the stars aligned, it would be my honor to ask exactly that." His smile faded. "Unfortunately, this isn't a social call. We need to talk." He motioned toward the opening. "Mind if I come in?"

"Oh, of course." She moved to the side and pulled open the door the rest of the way. "You're probably cold, and here I am running my mouth. I can get you a hot chocolate or a…" She stared at him in surprise when he immediately shut the door behind him and flipped the dead bolt.

A prickle of unease ran down her spine. "Okay, that's weird. First, a knock on the door with no one there. Then you show up and lock the door as if the devil's on your heels." She laughed awkwardly. "Is there an axe murderer on the loose in the Smoky Mountains that I should be on guard against?"

His intense gaze zeroed in on her. "Someone knocked on your door? Then hid?"

"Yes, I suppose, I mean…it sounded like knocking. But it could have been a bird or an animal making noise outside. I was just checking the peephole when you drove up."

His pistol was suddenly out, pointed down by his side. "Are all your windows and doors locked?"

"I, ah, I guess so. I mean, I haven't opened any of them since I got here. But—"

"Lock the door behind me. Wait here. Don't go outside." He was out the door, turning left and running toward the side of the cabin before she could stop him.

She shut the door harder than necessary and locked it as he'd told her. But when she started toward the couch, she stopped. "The heck with this. I didn't drive four hours to be treated like a helpless little woman. I get enough of that at work." She grabbed her pistol and headed outside.

Since Lance had gone left, she went right, hoping that if there was someone out here, she and Lance would corner them. It seemed a bit ridiculous having her pistol out, looking for what likely amounted to some teenager playing a game of doorbell ditch. Although there weren't any other cabins immediately nearby, there were some farther down this road. Definitely within walking distance if some kids wanted to play a prank on a tourist. But if Lance was concerned enough to pull his gun, she was going to follow his lead, at least until she found out why he was so worried.

As she continued around the side of the house, she didn't encounter any juvenile delinquents or anyone else. She didn't hear anyone either, or really much of anything. Other than a light cool breeze blowing through the branches overhead, making her long for her jacket, the woods were eerily silent. No squirrels chattering. No birds chirping. No rustling in the undergrowth as a raccoon or other small creature searched for food. She hesitated. Had it ever been like this since her arrival? It seemed as if there was always something making noise. Why was it so quiet now?

On high alert, she raised her pistol out in front of her, sweeping it back and forth as she checked the bushes near the cabin's foundation. To her left, she studied the thick undergrowth of the woods, looking for something that didn't quite belong. Listening for a potential threat.

Stopping at the back corner of the cabin, she ducked down. Keeping her head low, she peered around the corner through the maze of timbers driven deep into the slope of the mountain, anchoring the house to bedrock. Nothing. No rebellious teenagers. No bad guy hanging off a stilt, aiming a gun at her. But Lance wasn't there either. Shouldn't he have reached the other corner a few seconds before her?

Her stomach sank. Maybe he'd run into some trouble. And she was his only backup. She whirled around and jogged toward the front of the house.

It nearly killed her to stop at the corner. But running full tilt into the open without looking first was a newbie maneuver. With only six years in law enforcement, she didn't come close to matching the experience of those at UB. But she sure as heck wasn't a rookie.

Crouching down low again to make herself less of a target, she peered around the edge of the cabin toward the raised front porch. Empty. So where had Lance—

Crunching leaves sounded behind her. She jerked around. A man dressed in black dove at her from the trees. Before she could even react, he slammed against her, crushing her against the log wall of the cabin. Her gun flew from her grip, skittering across the ground. She twisted and clawed at his arms around her waist, furiously trying to break free.

He cursed in her ear and jerked her up in the air.

She raked her nails across both of his arms, but couldn't reach any skin through his long-sleeved black shirt. Clawing at his hands didn't work either. They were covered with leather gloves. Grabbing one of his gloved fingers, she yanked back, hard. A loud pop was followed by his shout of rage and pain.

He threw her against the cabin wall as if she were a rag doll. She slammed hard against it, letting out a yelp of pain as she fell to her knees. Her ribs hurt with every gasping breath. Her ears rang from the impact. But she couldn't just curl up in the fetal position. She had to push through the pain, defend herself. Where was her gun? Where?

He stood a few feet away, chest heaving from exertion, his injured hand clutched to his chest. Dressed completely in black, with a cloth covering the lower part of his face, all that showed were his dark brown eyes, staring at her with the promise of retribution.

Using his uninjured hand, he drew a long jagged knife from beneath his shirt.

"What do you want?" she demanded, desperately looking around. There, her pistol. It was about three feet away, half buried in some dried leaves.

He rushed toward her, knife raised high.

She rolled to the side, barely avoiding the swipe of his deadly blade. Then she dove for the pistol. His guttural yell sounded behind her. She let out a panicked whimper as she grabbed her gun and flipped onto her back.

Lance was suddenly there, tackling the man with the knife. They both fell onto the ground, locked together in a deadly embrace.

Keira leaped to her feet, her protesting ribs making

her breath catch. Stumbling, she pushed through the pain, bringing her gun up. But she couldn't get a clear shot.

She didn't need one.

The fight was over as quickly as it had begun. The man with the knife grunted and collapsed onto the ground, his own blade protruding from his neck. Blood quickly saturated his collar as he made a sickening gurgling sound.

Lance jerked his head up, eyes widening in alarm. "Keira, hit the deck!"

She threw herself to the ground.

Bam! Bam! Bam!

She gasped in shock as another man dressed in black fell to the ground a few yards from where she'd been standing. A gun skipped across the dirt from his lifeless hands. Lance had saved her. But why did she even need saving?

"What the heck is going on, Lance? Why did these men follow you here?"

"They didn't follow *me*. They followed *you*." He grabbed her hand. "Come on. We have to get out of here." He tugged her toward his SUV.

"What do you mean they followed me? The only people I've met around here are you and the others at UB."

"We'll figure it out later." He motioned toward the passenger side as he aimed his key fob at the vehicle. "Get in."

Gunshots echoed through the trees. Bullets shattered the rear window, raining glass across the concrete like pennies pinging against a metal pan.

He jerked back and fired toward the trees on the incline across the street. More bullets slammed into the back of the SUV.

Keira returned fire, aiming where she'd seen the flash of muzzle fire in the trees.

"Get in the cabin," Lance yelled. "I'll cover you."

"We'll cover each other."

He frowned, but didn't argue. They both fired their pistols toward the trees as they raced up the steps and charged into the house. This time, she was the one who slammed the door shut and flipped the lock. Lance pulled her to the floor beneath the front windows a few feet from the entryway. He covered her body with his as bullets slammed into the front door.

Keira shoved at him, her lungs straining for air beneath his tight hold even as her sore ribs screamed in pain. "You know I'm a cop, right?" she forced out, then dragged in another painful breath. "I can defend myself. Get off me."

"And you know I'm a man, right? And a former cop myself? I'm not going to cower while a woman takes a bullet for me."

She shoved at him, cursing.

He laughed. "Maybe you should have been a sailor. Those are some salty words coming out of that pretty mouth."

"You think this is funny?" She coughed, then dragged in another painful breath. "People are trying to kill us."

"Not the first time. Won't be the last." He cocked his head, listening, his weight still crushing her ribs. "The shooting has stopped."

She shoved against him again. "Good. Maybe they gave up."

"Don't count on it. Lucky for us that solid door and the log walls stopped the bullets. They're obviously not using high-powered rifles. Must be using handguns."

"And knives."

He grimaced. "And knives. I'm guessing we have a couple of minutes while they regroup and plan their entry."

"Then you really need to get off me. Now, before I faint from lack of oxygen."

He looked down, a wry grin on his face. "Sorry about that." He rolled off her but stayed on the floor beside her. "Don't stand up until we're clear of the windows."

"No kidding." She drew her first deep breath and immediately regretted it, grimacing in pain.

"What's wrong?" He slid a hand across her abdomen, then up toward her chest as if searching for wounds. "Did he cut you? Were you hit?"

She grabbed his hand before things got embarrassing. "No cuts. No bullet wounds. The guy outside threw me against the side of the cabin." She shoved his hand away. "I don't think anything's broken. Just bruised." She drew some quick, shallow breaths, relieved that the pain was much more bearable that way. Rolling slightly to her side, she slid her cell phone out of her jeans pocket.

He frowned. "What are you doing?"

"Calling 911."

"I'd rather not involve the police."

She gave him an incredulous look. "Seriously? I *am* the police. We're *already* involved."

He grinned. "Well, there is that. I don't suppose we really have an alternative at this point. I didn't expect them to move on you so fast."

She paused with her phone in her hand. "Move on me? That's the second time you've essentially said that I'm the target. Maybe it's you they're after."

"Oh, they are. No question. But they didn't know where I was until you led them to Gatlinburg, to Unfinished Business."

"You're blaming all of this on me?"

"Of course not. I was just explaining—"

A thumping sound came from above. They both looked up.

"They're on the roof," he said. "They're probably leery of trying the front windows, guessing we'll shoot if they do. Please tell me this place doesn't have a skylight."

"Kitchen, back left corner." She tapped the phone's screen, dialing 911. But when she put the phone to her ear, there was only static. She checked the phone to see if it had been damaged. It was pristine, not a single scratch. And there were four bars. Excellent reception. So why wasn't the call going through?

Lance grabbed the phone and held it to his ear. "Cell service is jammed."

"Jammed? What the—who *are* these people? What do they want?"

"At the moment? Both of us dead. Or, more likely, you dead and me alive long enough to be tortured for information. Then they'll kill me."

She stared at him in horror. "What did you do? Sleep with a mafia boss's daughter?"

He let out a bark of laughter. "I wish. At least then all of this might have been worth it."

"You're joking at a time like this?"

"I'm multitasking, trying to come up with a plan that involves both of us staying alive, minus the torture part."

"What's the plan?"

"Did you miss the *trying to come up with one* part?"

She rolled her eyes. "We need to get out of here. Hide somewhere."

"On that we agree. It's the how that I haven't figured out. Cabin layout?"

"Kitchen on the left, this family room, bedroom and bathroom through that door on the far right."

"What about the door beside the bedroom door? Closet?"

"Basement. The rec room. But there's no exit. No windows or doors. Solid concrete walls. We'd be trapped if we went down there."

"Those concrete walls will offer protection, with only one entrance to guard—the stairs. That's more than we have on this level."

"I don't like it," she said.

A loud bang sounded from the kitchen, followed by the sound of shattering glass.

Lance tightened his grip on his pistol. "Time to make our stand, General Custer. Outside, where the bullets were flying earlier? Or the basement without windows?"

"I'll take my chances outside." She jumped up to open the front door.

He tackled her back to the floor just before a barrage of gunfire shattered the window where she'd been standing, raining glass down on top of them.

She swore, grabbing the edge of a blanket from the back of a nearby chair and tossing it on the floor over the glass. Then she scrambled across it toward the front door.

He quickly followed, blocking her way so she wouldn't try to open the door. "About that plan—"

"I know, I know. As much as I hate it, the basement's our only viable option."

"Smart lady. *Go*." He pushed her ahead of him. They both crawled as fast as they could, knees bumping against the hard wood floors, staying low to avoid becoming a target through any of the windows.

They were almost to the basement door when shouts sounded behind them.

"Hurry," Lance yelled.

Keira jumped up and shoved the basement door open. The dark, constricted space below had her hesitating and drawing a painful, bracing breath to try to tamp down her fears. At Lance's questioning look, she straightened her shoulders, then forced herself to hurry down the stairs. At the bottom, she anxiously whirled around, expecting Lance to be right behind her. Instead, he stood silhouetted in the doorway above.

"Lock the door," he yelled, then slammed it shut. Something thumped against it.

She stood there, stunned. What the heck? She whipped out her pistol and raced back up the stairs. But when she pushed the door, it barely moved. She strained against it, only managing to open the door a few millimeters. That thump she'd heard. Lance must have shoved a chair or something else under the doorknob to keep her in the basement.

The fears from her past battered at her, narrowing her vision with darkness. She had to get out. She yelled some choice phrases at him and slammed her shoulder against the door. Her ribs protested the abuse, making her double over in pain. She drew small shaky breaths until she could straighten. Then she beat her fist against the wood, over and over, her whole body shaking. "Lance! Let me out!"

Gunshots sounded from the main room. Grunts. Shouts. More breaking glass. How many of those lunatics were out there? She shoved at the door over and over, fighting through the pain, desperate to get out to help Lance. And desperate to escape this dungeon before she curled into a fetal position like the terrified young girl she'd once been. Out. She had to get out!

A few agonizing minutes later, the sudden silence

shook her even more than the shouts and gunshots had. Was this the calm before the storm, like earlier when the birds had stopped chirping? What was going on?

The door yanked open.

She stumbled back, grabbing the railing to keep from falling as she swung her pistol toward the man looming there. He immediately raised his hands. Recognition slammed into her. She jerked her gun down.

"Mr. Prescott?"

"Officer Sloane." He dropped his hands, sounding slightly out of breath. There was a fresh cut on his jaw. His business suit was torn in several places. And his formerly white shirt was now dotted with blood. "At the risk of sounding cliché, the coast is clear."

Lance appeared beside him, looking far worse than his boss. Blood was smeared on his clothes, his neck, his hair. Bruises were already darkening along his jaw.

She rushed up the last few steps to the doorway. "Lance. Are you hurt? What—"

"We don't have much time," he said. "It's taken them twelve years to find me. Now that they have, they'll come at me with everything they've got. Anyone here when their reinforcements arrive is in danger." He held his hand out to Keira. "We're leaving. Now."

She shoved her pistol into the waistband of her pants and brushed past him into the main room. Her eyes widened when she saw the destruction and death around her. Several men dressed in black lay crumpled on the floor in various locations, clearly beyond help. Asher, Ryland, Faith and two other UB investigators stood near the stone fireplace at the back of the family room, looking as disheveled as their boss, several of them bleeding from various cuts.

"What happened?" she asked. "Have any of you been seriously hurt?"

Lance shoved a fresh magazine into his pistol as he peered out the back windows looking up at the mountains.

Grayson stopped beside Keira. "Thankfully, everyone's okay. Lance got the worst of it. He was fighting two men at once when we got here."

Lance turned from the windows. "I had it under control. You shouldn't have come."

"You're welcome." Grayson rolled his eyes.

Lance let out a deep breath and glanced at his teammates, offering a quick nod of thanks. As he stepped over to Keira and Grayson, he flipped back his suit jacket and shoved his pistol into the holster on his belt. "I don't mean to sound ungrateful. But I'd really hoped to not involve any of you in this. How did you know where I was? Or that Keira might be in trouble?"

Asher motioned to the destruction around them. "We all got to talking after you left. You were really defensive during the meeting, trying far too hard to discredit Officer Sloane's investigation. It was obvious there was something going on and that it involved both of you. Figuring out what cabin she'd rented only took a few calls. We'd planned on coming over to talk to her first, then we were going to your place. We didn't expect to get caught at the O.K. Corral."

Keira put her hands on her hips. "What's going on, Lance? You said these men have been after you for years but that they followed me. Did it occur to you that you could have warned me earlier in the safety of UB's conference room?"

His dark brooding gaze locked on hers. "Nothing you told me in the meeting made me think you'd attracted the attention of these guys. I came here to talk, to make absolutely sure you hadn't done anything to put yourself at risk. And then I was going to try to convince you to drop the case, to *keep* you out of danger. If I'd known they'd followed you, that they were in Gatlinburg, I sure as hell wouldn't have let you walk into an ambush. I'd have taken you with me when I left UB and protected you."

"Hold it," Faith said. "Do I have this right? Someone's been trying to find you and kill you for *years*. Rick Cameron is somehow involved. And you were worried that Keira may have led these enemies to you. Yet, instead of telling us about it and asking us to help, you risked your life, and hers, by trying to handle this alone?"

Lance winced. "It sounds way worse when you put it like that."

Asher stepped closer to him. "You had an odd look on your face in the war room when you told me you'd see me later. You were lying, weren't you? When you left UB, you were leaving for good, not planning on ever coming back. Tell me I'm wrong, Lance. Please, for God's sake, tell me I'm wrong."

Lance looked away.

Asher swore.

Keira pulled out her cell phone.

"Don't tell me you're trying to call the police again." Lance sounded alarmed.

"Assuming the cell signal isn't still jammed, dang straight I'm calling the police."

He grabbed her phone. *"No."*

Grayson motioned toward the others. Suddenly Keira and Lance were surrounded by the UB investigators, a wall of men and one woman—Faith—blocking them from leaving.

"The police are already on their way," Grayson told him. "And you're not going anywhere without telling your teammates, your friends, what exactly is going on."

Lance looked like he wanted to argue, but the sound of sirens coming up the mountain had him fisting his hands by his sides.

Grayson put his hand on Lance's shoulder. "I can practically see the wheels spinning in your mind, trying to weave some kind of story to make us leave you alone. You're trying to figure out how to keep all of us safe while you, and potentially Officer Sloane too, face something incredibly dangerous on your own. These obviously aren't your run-of-the-mill criminals out to settle a score. They appear to be highly organized, trained and well funded. You need our help, whether you want it or not."

Lance's jaw tightened. "I don't want any of you hurt." He glanced around at them, then let out a shaky breath. "Any more hurt than you already are."

Grayson dropped his hand from Lance's shoulder. "I don't want that either. Which is why you need to level with us, give us information so we know who we're fighting against. Then we'll fight them together." He looked at the others. "Am I right?"

"Damn straight," Faith said, her words echoed by the team.

Keira arched a brow at Lance and raised her voice to be heard over the approaching sirens. "I'm already in this. And I'm not letting you leave without me."

Grayson motioned toward the front windows, or what was left of them after being shattered by bullets. "Gatlinburg PD is going to pull up out front any minute now. Lance, give me your word that you're going to work with us, that you'll explain everything, and we'll come up with a plan together. No playing this solo."

He gave all of them a pained look, then nodded. "All right. I'll tell you everything. But not in front of the police."

"The police can help us," Grayson argued.

"Not with this. Trust me."

He stared at Lance a few moments, then nodded. "All right. I'll accept that, for now. But we've got to come up with a cover story. Fast."

"Sticking close to the truth works best," Keira said. "Less chance of our stories not matching. That should be easy since Lance is the only one in this room who knows what's going on and who is after him."

He gave her an odd look, as if he were going to correct something she'd said. Instead, he shrugged and remained silent.

"Sirens have stopped." Faith motioned toward the jagged openings where the front windows used to be. "I don't see the police, so they've likely parked down the street in case there are active gunmen. But they're probably running through the woods toward the cabin as we speak. Keira's right. We should stick to the truth where we can. We can honestly say that we all came here to see Keira and were surprised that Lance was here too and that these ninja guys were trying to kill them. But how do we explain Keira being here in Gatlinburg? Why we were coming to see her? Or you, Lance, coming to see her, without us bringing up Rick Cameron's case and whatever it has to do with your mysterious past?"

"That part's easy." Lance gave Keira a half smile and put his arm around her shoulders. "You and I are dating. My friends found out this morning when I told them at

UB. After I left, they came over to see you, to push for information about our relationship. I, of course, was already here, you being my girlfriend and all."

Her cheeks flushed and she pushed his arm off her shoulder. "Try to kiss me and I'll punch you."

His grin widened. "Noted."

Movement caught their attention out front. Police in flak jackets emerged from the cover of the trees, boots thumping as they raced up the porch stairs and aimed long guns through the openings.

Lance swore.

"Gatlinburg PD," one of them yelled. "Drop any weapons you have. Come out with your hands up."

Grayson straightened his suit jacket, frowning at the drops of blood and rips in the expensive fabric. "Everyone say as little as possible." He spoke low so those out front wouldn't hear him. "Stick to the story Lance just made up. Don't offer any extra information." He shook his head as if in disgust. "May God help us all. We're about to lie to the chief of police."

Chapter Five

In all her twenty-eight years, other than the awful things that had happened during her teen years, Keira couldn't think of a single day that was crazier, scarier, more frustrating, painful or confusing than today had been. And it wasn't close to being over. The sun was only just now beginning to set. But instead of being warm and cozy in her cabin as she'd planned when she first woke up, she was back at Unfinished Business.

One of the differences between this morning and now was that instead of being in a conference room, she was sitting in a chair in the middle of the so-called war room. Chairs had been arranged in a large circle. But few of them were occupied. The UB investigators were standing around in small groups talking, drinking and eating sandwiches their boss had ordered for their dinner.

The biggest difference from this morning was her reason for being here. She wasn't just looking into a cold case now. She was trying to find out why she'd been shot at, beaten, almost stabbed, locked in a dark basement and, perhaps worst of all, been forced to lie to fellow police officers. Rather than tell them she was here to investigate a murder, she'd told them she was Lance's girlfriend.

As if something like that could ever happen. She couldn't

imagine the stars ever aligning between them, not after their inauspicious start.

Making everything worse was that she'd been blackmailed at the cabin by Gatlinburg's police chief Russo to go to the hospital. She'd argued that she knew her ribs were only bruised, not broken. *After all, she'd had broken ribs before.* Of course, she hadn't shared that information with him. Still, it was only because Russo threatened to call her boss to order her to the hospital that she'd finally given in.

Now here she was, with bruised, not broken, ribs—as she'd predicted. And instead of being happy and grateful to have some tips and suggestions from a group of experienced investigators like she had been earlier, she was now desperate to find out how she could avoid the same fate as Rick Cameron.

She glanced around the room. Everyone who'd been at the cabin sported bandages or stitches on their various cuts and scrapes. Lance by far had the most injuries, with stitches on both forearms, his left calf and his scalp. Keira considered herself lucky that she'd only sustained a few minor abrasions. And that it only hurt when she breathed. Okay, maybe that wasn't something to exactly be thankful for. But considering how much worse it could have been, she wasn't complaining. Especially since none of her cuts had required stitches.

She hated needles.

And doctors.

And hospitals.

All they did was bring up bad memories.

Chief Russo had no way of knowing that. But it didn't keep him from being added to her list of people she'd rather avoid in the future. After all, it was only because of him that flashbacks of her childhood kept parading like a horror movie in her mind's eye. She didn't need that added stress on top of everything else, not today.

Impatient for everyone to join the circle so they could start the discussion, she looked past them through the two-story windows that overlooked the front parking lot.

Where the asphalt ended, the scary, twisty two-lane road up and down the mountain began. Just past that, the mountain rose steeply, its peak one of the tallest in the Smokies. From what she'd been told, the road ended at the very top of this particular mountain, at Grayson Prescott's estate. And since the mountain was called Prescott Mountain, she could only assume he owned the whole darn thing. How incredible was that?

Even if she ever had the money to afford it, she wouldn't want a mountain. Her multitude of fears from claustrophobia to heights and a ridiculously long list of other things would keep her from wanting to travel up and down a winding road every day. But, man oh man, could she appreciate the natural beauty around here.

Even in the fading sunlight, the scenery was so surreal that it made her want to stare out the windows and forget everything else around her. Tall, spindly oaks devoid of leaves marched up the steep slope beside thick, dark evergreens. Jagged rocks in varying shapes and sizes jutted out at odd angles, catching the light and forming a tapestry of colors that would make an artist weep. It was so much more picturesque than flat Maple Falls. But what struck her the most were the little puffs of white mist that gave the mountains their name—the Smokies.

When she'd first visited the Great Smoky Mountains National Park as a small child, she'd been terrified at the white puffs, convinced that the woods were on fire.

Thankfully, her mom knew otherwise and had reassured her. Those were the good times, when her family had been a real family. Before her father had turned to alcohol and painkillers to drown his guilt. Before everything had gone so horribly wrong.

"Never seen a mountain before?" Lance sat beside her. The teasing note in his voice was tempered by the lines of worry on his forehead.

"Not in a very long time."

His gaze sharpened, the lines of worry deepening. "That sounded ominous. What's wrong?"

"Other than someone wanting to kill me?"

"Don't."

"Don't what?"

"Lie to me. Don't pretend that you were thinking about the mess we're in. Something else was on your mind, something that put haunting shadows in your eyes. What is it? Something from your past? You seemed so lost, a million miles away." He gently took one of her hands in his and turned it over, revealing the ugly scars. "Is this part of it? The reason for the shadows?"

Her breath caught and she snatched her hand back, curling her fingers against her palms to cover the angry red welts. She forced a laugh. "Haunting shadows? Really? When did you become a poet?"

He didn't crack a smile. Instead, he simply waited, as if he expected her to confess her deepest, darkest secrets.

That was never going to happen.

"If by something in my past you mean being attacked by ninjas," she scoffed, "then you're right on target. Yes, my past…my *recent* past is bothering me. When do we get to hear the truth about what's going on? The truth about *your* past?"

He studied her, his expression turning sad. Or was it more that he was…disappointed?

Finally, he shrugged and motioned to the others. "As soon as everyone's settled—" his voice was raised so the team could hear him "—I'll start."

The little groups broke apart. The newest arrivals grabbed their laptops or computer tablets and hurried to take their seats. Faith and her husband, Asher, were already sitting across from Lance and Keira. Ryland, the team lead, was next to Faith. The other two men from the cabin sat close by. They had been reintroduced to Keira as Trent and Callum since she had forgotten their names from the earlier meeting.

The remaining members of the UB investigative team were here too, with the exception of their boss, Grayson, and his wife, Willow. They were both at the police station, where Grayson was trying to placate the chief. There'd been no way to hide what had happened from the media with so many gunshots and the destruction at the cabin. Not to mention the body bags being carried out to coroner's vans. The chief wasn't letting this go with a simple "home invasion" explanation.

Apparently he was a close friend of Grayson's, and he was also Willow's former boss. Their history together was the only reason the rest of them were allowed to leave the hospital after being treated without enduring lengthy police interviews. But they'd had to agree to go to the station later for more questioning if Grayson wasn't able to satisfy Russo with his answers.

Once everyone was seated and quiet descended upon the room, every eye turned to Lance. This man whom Keira viewed as the epitome of confidence and decisiveness now seemed uncertain, hesitant. After briefly glancing around the circle at his fellow investigators and Keira, he drew a deep breath and began to speak.

"Officer Sloane, I mean Keira, and all of my friends here at Unfinished Business, everything you think you know about me is a lie."

Chapter Six

Lance would rather face a roomful of gunmen with only a pistol and one magazine of ammo to defend himself than the people sitting around this circle. He cared deeply for them, and even felt a deep connection to Keira. After all, she'd been through hell because his past had followed her to Gatlinburg. His biggest regret was that he was responsible for putting both her and his work family in danger. Because of his actions, or inaction, he was about to lose the friendship of everyone in this room.

On the opposite side of the circle of chairs, Faith gave him an encouraging smile. "Come on, Lance. We know you. You can't fake the stuff that really matters, the kind of person you are. That comes out in actions, not words. So whatever it is that you've been hiding, don't be afraid to share. We're all friends here, family really." She smiled at Keira. "And future friends. We can't fix this unless we know what's going on."

He grimaced. "Some things aren't fixable."

Keira surprised him by briefly squeezing his hand. "We can at least try."

He smiled, but he already knew this meeting wasn't going to help. And he still wasn't committed to fully disclosing everything in spite of his promise to Grayson. It was too dangerous.

"As I said, everything you think you know about me is a lie, starting with my name. Lance Cabrera is the alias I took on twelve years ago. My birth name is Lance Mitchell." When the huge outcry he'd expected didn't happen, he hesitated, frowning. "I don't come from out west like I've led you all to believe. My hometown is in central Florida, a city called Gainesville. My résumé that I used to join Unfinished Business is a fabrication."

Ryland shook his head, his gaze locked on Lance. "No. It isn't. I recruited you. You were working as a detective in Nashville. I visited you there at your job. Spoke to your peers, your boss. He gave you a glowing recommendation, said you were the best detective he'd worked with in his forty-year career. Are you saying he made all that up? That he allowed a civilian to pretend to be a detective the day I was there?"

"Well, no, of course not. He told the truth as he saw it. I worked for Nashville PD for over eight years."

"As Lance Cabrera."

"Yes."

"Then if you're expecting shock or recriminations from us because you changed your name prior to that, you'll be disappointed. People change their names for all kinds of reasons. Heck, Faith changed her last name from Lancaster to Whitfield when she married Asher. We still consider her to be a friend, more or less."

Faith made a rude gesture.

Ryland grinned. "My point, Lance, is that we already know from what happened this morning and what little you've told us so far, that something bad in your past has caught up to you. If I felt that changing my name would help me get a much-needed fresh start, I wouldn't hesitate. What we need to know is who these people are and why they're after you." He motioned toward Keira. "And why they went after Officer Sloane. Stop worrying about how we'll feel and give us the facts. Tell us what we're up against. Then we'll all deal with the fallout. All right, brother?"

Lance was shocked at the nods of agreement from everyone in the room, including Keira. He hadn't expected that. He offered up one last warning. "I appreciate the support, more than you know. But if we continue, if I tell you everything, it puts all of you in danger. As it is, it will be difficult to put a slant on whatever stories the media is already spinning, to placate the bad guys. We need to make it convincing that UB being at the cabin truly has nothing to do with my past. Doing that should keep you all safe. Keira and I can leave and deal with this alone. My primary concern for her is to figure out how she got involved in this and find a way to get her out of it. The rest is on me to handle."

Ryland shook his head again. "No way. You aren't facing this alone. You've saved my life on numerous occasions, plus a few more of us. You were part of the team that helped save Asher on his last big case. We owe you for that."

"You've saved my life too," Lance argued. "You owe me nothing."

"Then consider this," Ryland said. "As far as I'm concerned, we're family. Family doesn't run when one of theirs is in trouble. Not this family anyway. Am I right guys?"

"And gals," Faith and Ivy chimed in, laughing because they'd both said the same thing.

Faith smiled. "We are family, Lance. And Keira is too, because her fate is apparently tied with yours, at least right now. None of us is running away from this, no matter how hard you try to convince us."

Everyone voiced their agreement.

Lance let out a shuddering breath, his throat tight. He'd never met a group of better people. And while he didn't want to involve them any more than they already were, it was clear they weren't going to give him that choice. All he could do now was prepare them.

He nodded his thanks, and when he'd composed himself enough to speak again, he began his story.

"To understand what's happening, I have to start where this began for me, my senior year in college. My on-again, off-again girlfriend, Ileana Sanchez, was off-again. Thankfully she was majoring in IT, computer programming, and I was following the criminology track. With radically different majors, the only times we crossed each other's paths was at sporting events or the restaurants on campus. I was just a few months shy of graduation.

"Most of my classmates were applying for jobs with police departments, hoping to move up the ladder from beat cop to detective eventually. I was determined to start out right away doing what I loved, solving mysteries, figuring out whodunit. I didn't want to spend years earning my stripes and paying my dues. My naive, overinflated ego had me applying for jobs with the big dogs—FBI, CIA, Homeland Security, you name it. If it was an agency with a glitzy reputation, I tried to get in."

Trent chuckled. "Ambition with a capital A. Those places prefer their candidates to have real-world experience in other careers or agencies before signing on with them. I imagine you got turned down flat."

"You'd be right," Lance said, "with one exception. A man I'd never met—Ian Murphy—working for an agency

I'd never heard of contacted me. He said he had been given my name from one of those other agencies. But who he got it from exactly, and how, was vague. He never quite explained that part."

"Red flags, buddy," Trent said.

"Where were you when I was naive and twenty-two, Trent?"

Trent laughed. "Just as young and naive as you, I'm guessing."

Lance smiled. "The sales pitch was incredible. The agency was brand-new, super secret and flush with money. They wanted young, energetic, smart people who would bridge the gap between the rules the law enforcement entities were forced to abide by versus what civilians could get away with. An example he gave me was that the FBI might not be able to secure a warrant they need in order to conduct some kind of surveillance because a judge doesn't agree that they have probable cause. But there's nothing stopping a civilian from performing his own surveillance and passing along any evidence he obtains. It provides the FBI with something tangible to convince a judge to give them a warrant. But it doesn't quite cross the line that would get the evidence thrown out. It's a legal loophole. Murphy was tasked with exploiting that loophole to help ensure the safety and security of the American people and our country. I was practically foaming at the mouth to sign up."

Keira nodded. "They appealed to your patriotism and the idealism a young man would have, not being jaded yet from the real world."

"They definitely knew which buttons to push. But, honestly, I was more excited about the prospect of getting to be a detective right out of the gate. The money he offered wasn't anything to sneeze at either. And once my ex-girlfriend got wind of the job offer I was considering, she was suddenly flirting with me again. I was too stupid to realize it was the money, not me, that she wanted."

Ryland shook his head in commiseration. "She must have been really hot."

Lance laughed. "She wasn't bad to look at, that's for sure. And I was still young enough and shallow enough that I liked having a beautiful woman on my arm, regardless of whether we got along well or not."

Keira rolled her eyes. "Was she blonde?"

"Ouch," Faith complained, pointing to her long blond hair.

"Sorry." Keira's face reddened.

"No, she wasn't blonde," Lance answered, smiling. "She had Spanish heritage and used that to her advantage. She'd never have dreamed of coloring her dark hair. It was her pride and joy." He shook his head. "Anyway, my point is, you can see the allure of the job offer on many levels, and I jumped at it.

"We took huge risks every day, putting our lives on the line with the bad guys we were after. And there was a risk that if we crossed a line too far, we might end up getting arrested. If that ever happened, we were sworn to secrecy. If we said it was part of our job, our employer would deny even knowing us. The agency's cover was that it was a private-eye service. And that's what they'd stick to, denying we even worked for them. We'd be completely on our own. Since I never expected to get caught, I wasn't worried. And since I made more money in one month than most police detectives make in a year, I had no intention of heeding the little warning bells that kept going off in the back of my mind. The money was a powerful incentive to someone fresh out of school. I paid off my student loans in the first six months of the job."

Asher whistled. "It took me a decade to pay mine off. I can see the appeal of working for this place. What was it called? Are they still in operation?"

"It was a nondescript front in a strip mall in a tiny central Florida town called Ocala. The official name is Ocala Private Investigations, or OPI. If there was an official government name for the agency, we never knew about it. Everything was on a need-to-know basis. Each of us knew a different piece of the overall puzzle. But no one knew it all, except our boss. As to your second question, OPI went out of business years ago."

Keira motioned for his attention. "Since you're focusing on this OPI, can you confirm they're the ones behind what happened this morning? That's where you're heading, isn't it?"

"Yes and no. OPI was the catalyst for everything that went wrong. But I don't have any proof that they're the ones behind what happened."

"What *did* happen?" Keira asked.

"After a handful of years working there, I was the team lead over eight other people—seven men, one woman. We were given a complicated mission that required the whole team. Each of us was supposed to develop dossiers on people whose names we were given. They weren't ordinary, everyday people with their lives plastered on social media. It was tough getting any information on them and took a lot of surveillance work. But we did it and gave the files to our boss. From there, he handed them off to his contact at the appropriate alphabet agency. Job done. Move on to the next assignment. Only, that's not exactly what happened."

He rested his forearms on his thighs and clasped his hands together, forming a fist as he thought back. "The very next day, I was surfing the internet and stumbled onto a routine story about some person getting mugged and killed that morning. The police were asking for any witnesses to come forward. When I saw the name of the victim, it sent ice-cold chills down my spine. It was one of the people whom I'd investigated. I'd given his file to my boss the night before."

Keira's eyes widened "Are you sure it was the same person? Maybe someone else had the same name?"

"I'd hoped that very thing. But it didn't take long to confirm it was the same person. I told my boss. He assured me it had to be a coincidence and to not worry about it. But it kept niggling at me. I couldn't let it go. I created some automated searches on the internet to alert me if more coincidences happened. A week later, I got a hit."

"Another person on the list was killed?" Keira asked.

Lance nodded, clasping his hands so tightly his knuckles ached. "Not just one." He glanced at his team. "All of them. There were nine people we'd investigated in that most recent assignment. In the span of one week, every single one of them was dead. Each alone didn't seem suspicious—random accidents, common health ailments like a heart attack, nothing particularly concerning. But together, it was a pattern. An incredibly disturbing pattern. One that I reported to Murphy. He glossed it over again, seemed uninterested. But I couldn't ignore it."

Asher leaned forward in his chair. "You dug into your other cases, didn't you? To see if anything like that had happened before."

Lance nodded grimly. "As you might guess, it had. Nothing recent. In fact, most of our cases were proven to be on the up and up. We found where cases we'd worked ended up going to trial and the guilty parties went to prison. The evidence we'd collected, things like recordings of people in bars or other public places spilling their secrets, most of it went to a good cause. Or so we told ourselves. We rarely did anything outrageous enough to truly cross any lines, at least, not any lines on the civilian side of things."

He shook his head and sat back, stretching his legs out in front of him. "But as we dug back over the years, we found a disturbing number of people that we'd investigated had turned up dead within days of us turning in our information. Needless to say, we were stunned. All of us had spent years thinking we were helping people and getting rich in the process. But in reality, we were being used to hurt people. It didn't take much of a leap to realize other information we'd passed along probably wasn't used for legit purposes either. We were devastated."

Trent shook his head. "Man. That sucks."

"That's putting it mildly," Lance said.

"What did you do?" Keira asked, caught up in the story. "Did you go to your boss again?"

"We did. The whole team so he couldn't blow it off this time. We'd gathered all of our data on the suspicious cases and presented it in a meeting with him one morning. He couldn't deny it in front of him in black and white. And, honestly, he didn't try to. He seemed as shocked and disgusted as we were. He told us to give him twenty-four hours to contact the right people and get the ball rolling on figuring out who was behind this abuse of power. The assumption was that one of his liaisons was a mole, a dirty agent. Three hours later, Ian Murphy was dead. He was killed in a drive-by shooting in a restaurant parking lot. The police theory was that it was a gang member who mistook him for someone else. The actual shooter was never caught."

Asher scoffed. "Sounds fishy, to say the least."

Keira nodded.

"I'll cut to the point," Lance said. "In the next few weeks, one of our teammates, Allen Stanford, was also killed. Single car accident. Ran his car into a tree. No witnesses. His blood alcohol level was twice the legal limit. But here's the catch. Allen didn't drink. Ever. Someone staged his murder to look like an accident, not realizing he'd sworn off alcohol for personal reasons. A few weeks later, another team member, Brett Foster, was framed for a crime he didn't commit. While he was in jail waiting for bail to be set, he was shanked by another prisoner. He didn't die. But it was close."

"Let me guess," Ryland said, "the prisoner who shanked him was later shanked himself."

"Close enough," Lance said. "He was found hanging in his cell. Apparently, he committed suicide even though he was slated to be released the following week."

Ryland swore. "This is crazy scary. Your team was falling like dominoes."

"It doesn't stop there either. Now we get to Rick Cameron."

"We already know what happened to him," Keira said. "He was beaten and shot in his motel room."

Lance nodded. "But there's more. Before that, when OPI was falling apart, he too was framed for a crime he didn't commit. That's when we all agreed we were on someone's hit list and needed to do something drastic if we were going to survive. We bailed Rick out of jail, picked up our other friend from the hospital where he was recovering from being stabbed, and disappeared. We took on new identities, which in this post-9/11 world was no easy feat. And we went our separate ways. Rick's birth name was Rick Parker. Cameron was his new identity."

"What about your families?" Keira asked. "And your girlfriend? Did you leave them behind?"

"We did. Breaking up with Ileana was the best part of it for me, for both of us really. We were never healthy for each other, fought more often than not. I'd broken up with her many times. But she was gone for a few weeks, sometimes longer, then she always came back and managed to convince me to try again. This time, after I explained that I'd quit my job and that my massive paycheck was no longer going to be coming in, she didn't argue. She left. And since I went underground, I haven't seen her since. Though even if I hadn't gone on the run, I doubt she'd have tried to rekindle our relationship. She loved the money far more than she'd ever cared about me." He shrugged. "And I obviously didn't care for her the way I should have, considering how long we'd been together. Rather than pine for her, I was relieved the drama was finally over."

"Good riddance," Keira murmured.

"A hundred percent," Lance said. "The part that was really difficult was leaving our families. We considered it our duty, like joining the Witness Security Program, WitSec. We were forced to let go of our past so that we could protect the ones we loved." He gave her a baleful look. "I haven't seen or spoken to my parents, sister or brother since."

Keira swallowed, her eyes looking suspiciously bright. "From your expression, you must have really loved them."

The wonder in her tone confused him. It was as if she

couldn't fathom actually loving your family. Didn't she have a family who loved her?

"What about your team?" Keira asked. "The OPI team. Have you kept in touch with them? Is that what happened to Rick? Someone traced an email or phone call from an OPI teammate back to him?"

He locked away the questions she'd raised in his mind about her family and focused on their current, dire situation. "I can't imagine Rick being that careless. The story I've given all of you is a pared down version of everything that went on. There were other close calls. We didn't know who to trust. Every time we tried to pursue this so-called mole, to find out who was behind everything, an attempt would be made on one of our lives. The only reason more of us weren't killed was because we were hypervigilant, fully aware that someone very powerful with a lot to lose was after us. Believe me, if we could have outed them and put a stop to what they were doing, we would have. But we didn't have the resources, the ability. Going underground was our only choice. We all agreed we wouldn't call, email or contact each other in any way. That's how it's been ever since."

Faith frowned at him. "Rick was far closer to Gatlinburg when he was murdered than to his home in Louisiana. It's only logical that he found out you were in danger and was trying to reach you when he was killed. He must have given them your name and location. That's why the bad guys went after you, after Keira."

Lance was shaking his head before she finished. "We never shared our aliases or locations. We each kept our first name, but not our last. And we all moved away from Florida, not telling each other where we'd gone. Even if Rick was tortured for current information on his OPI team, he couldn't have told them what he doesn't know."

Keira stared at him, her eyes narrowed. "There's more to it. There has to be. You said they followed me to Gatlinburg, then to you. But I came here because Rick left that note and mentioned your name. He must have been in Maple Falls because he'd figured out where you were, thus the note. And he was on his way here to see you, maybe to warn you that the past was catching up."

Lance shrugged. "I believe you're partially right. Rick must have figured out where I was and felt he needed to come warn me. But he didn't want to put me in danger by trying to contact me in any way that could be traced."

"But he must have done something for them to know where you were."

"They didn't know where I was until they followed you to Gatlinburg, then to UB. Otherwise, when they'd killed Rick weeks ago, they'd have come straight here. Something else happened in Maple Falls, something you uncovered or did without even realizing it. That's why they followed you here. Was there any time when you told someone else about the words 'unfinished business' and my name? Maybe someone was watching you and the others involved in the investigation and saw, read or heard something substantive about the case."

"No way. We didn't know anything to tell. And I'm the only one who connected you to the note. The only one I told about that was Rick." She gave him a half smile. "I visited his grave on my way out of town, told him that I was trying to…" Her eyes widened. "Oh no."

"Go ahead," Lance urged her. "What are you remembering?"

She clutched her hands against her middle as if she

were feeling sick. "I spoke out loud to him, mentioned that I was going to find his killer and get him justice. I said I'd take care of his unfinished business and see if this Lance guy was his Lance guy."

"Were you alone?"

"I thought I was. But literally right after I said that out loud, I heard something in the woods. I thought it was an animal rooting around in the dried leaves. But I was spooked enough to take out my pistol until I was in my car."

"That's it," he said. "Must be. Someone was watching you and heard enough to think you knew where I was."

She put her hand on his forearm. "I'm so sorry. I had no idea."

He gently took her hand in his. "Of course you didn't. I'm grateful you figured out where I was. At least now I know someone is actively hunting my team again." When he would have let go, she held on for another moment.

"I really am sorry I put you in danger, Lance."

He gently squeezed her hand. "You did me a favor. Now that I know they're here, I can do what I need to do to protect myself. And you. We have to figure out how to extricate you from all this so you can return to Maple Falls without living in fear that they'll go after you."

This time, it was Keira who let go, pulling her hand back to clasp it tightly with the other, her face pale.

Lance was about to try to reassure her when Ryland spoke.

"The key to this seems to be in figuring out how Rick knew where you were. Any ideas on that?"

"I have a few, one in particular. It goes back to three months ago, when yet another one of my old teammates from OPI was murdered."

"Oh no," Keira said. "I'm so sorry."

He nodded his thanks.

"How did you find that out?" Ryland said, continuing to press for information.

"As you might imagine, being a team lead yourself, I've always felt responsible for my old team. I couldn't figure out the identity of whoever killed our boss and has tried to pick off each of us. So the least I could do was try to look out for them, in some way, without endangering them."

The pained look in Ryland's eyes confirmed that he well understood the feeling of responsibility and the guilt whenever any of them ran into trouble.

"One of the ways I've tried to do that is to set up automated searches of the internet. Every story that goes through the major news outlets, like Associated Press, gets fed into my searches. The first names of my team go through an algorithm I set up, something we used at OPI actually. It compares known details about my team with the news stories and uses a decision tree to determine whether to alert me via email. One of the most accurate parts of the decision tree that produces alerts is when pictures are involved. The algorithm uses facial recognition software. Three months ago, one of the searches found a picture of one of my old team members, Levi, with a reported last name of Alexander. Not his original birth name of course, but it was definitely him. He'd been killed in a mugging in New York. Most people aren't killed during muggings, so it wasn't typical. But there wasn't anything obvious to link it to our time at OPI either. But since then, I've been more aware and careful, keeping a lookout for signs that I'm being watched, followed."

"Man, that's a lot of baggage and stress to live with for so long," Asher said.

Lance shrugged, not feeling particularly worthy of any commiseration. Not when two of his teammates had been murdered in the past few months and he'd been unable to prevent their deaths.

"It's smart to keep tabs on your team as best you can," Ryland said. "But if you can use that kind of technology, especially the facial recognition searches, so can your enemies."

"Which is one of the reasons we've all agreed to steer clear of the media in any way so our photos aren't plastered on the internet. It's why I typically avoid photo ops on our cases, if you haven't noticed."

Faith nodded. "We've noticed. We figured you were one of those people who was camera shy."

He arched a brow. "*Shy* isn't in my vocabulary."

She laughed. "Okay, okay. We assumed you had your reasons. But now that you've explained it, that makes sense. You can't possibly avoid cameras all the time though. Airports alone will have you on their video systems from the moment you drive onto their property."

"It's a risk, for sure. Luckily, that post-9/11 security I mentioned earlier is top-notch on airport online systems, if not their physical security. I've flown many times and haven't found any photos of me from the security scans leaked to the internet. My algorithm searches for stories about me too, just in case something pops up, so I can try to take it down. So far, I haven't been targeted. Until today of course. But I also haven't done anything to stir up trouble. None of us has. So maybe that's the bigger reason why we haven't been found."

"Until three months ago," Keira said.

He winced. "Until three months ago. I've wondered if maybe Rick has done the same thing as me over the years.

He could have been running his own searches and saw that story about Levi. If he decided to go to New York to look into what happened, he could have been spotted, assuming the mole had seen the story and went there to see if any old OPI team members showed up. Rick could have been on the run since then, maybe after a close call. And he started digging, trying to find me, as the old team lead, so we could figure out what to do. And how to warn our other teammates. But they found him before he got to me."

Lance looked around, making sure that everyone was paying attention. "All of you who were at the cabin today saw the manpower the mole sent after Keira and me. There were a couple of guys outside, a few more who got into the cabin—"

"Eight total," Asher said.

Lance winced. "All heavily armed, trained and wearing identical outfits to conceal their features from any potential witnesses. From what I heard of the police talking to each other as they checked everything out, none of the bodies had ID. Ryland, I assume that you've been communicating with Grayson off and on today. Heard anything about any of the bad guys being identified?"

He shook his head. "Nothing at all. None of their fingerprints have come up as a match in any databases so far. AFIS will take a while. The FBI database checks always take longer than our local ones. Gatlinburg PD will check DNA too. But that'll take a while unless Grayson can convince them to use our lab, which isn't snowed under with queued up requests. But from everything you've said, I don't expect any matches on any criminal DNA databases, certainly not CODIS. No way would this mole hire someone with past arrests or convictions that would mean their DNA has been logged. He's got too much at stake for that."

"Agreed," Lance said. "This guy, or gal, running this operation has access to significant resources. And I don't have any clue as to his or her identity. That was the problem twelve years ago, and it's still the problem today."

The atmosphere in the room had gone somber and tense. Everyone appeared to be trying to absorb everything that Lance had said. It was finally sinking in that this was far more serious, and deadly, than anything they'd ever faced.

He rested his forearms on his knees again. "My OPI boss and three members of my old team have been murdered. It's possible more of them have been killed and I don't know about it. Assuming that hasn't happened, I have five teammates left. And I need to find every one of them to warn them. All of us from OPI need to change our aliases again, start over, again. On top of that, I need to figure out how to get Keira off the mole's radar so this doesn't destroy her life and force her to go underground too."

Lance gave her a weak smile. "I'm so sorry about all of this. But I swear to you that I'll do everything in my power to keep you safe, and get your life back."

She gave him a weak smile but was clearly upset.

"What's your plan?" Ryland asked. "It sounds as if you've made some decisions."

"My first priority is to get Keira somewhere safe where she can lay low. After that, I'll work on finding my team and warning them. Then I'm going to figure out once and for all who this mole is. I'm going to end this."

"No." Keira's brows were drawn down in a frown. "For one thing, you can't do this by yourself. It's impossible. And I'm not hiding out while you face this alone."

"Keira, with all due respect for your experience and

abilities as a police officer, you're not ready for this sort of thing. And more importantly, this isn't your fight."

"It became my fight the moment those maniacs tried to kill me. I want to bring them down as much as you. I made a promise to a dying man who entrusted your safety into my hands by telling me your name. That's sacred. I'm not running. I'm sticking with you. And I won't be a liability. I'll be your wingman or woman or whatever. Besides—" she gave him a saucy look "—you're not dumping your new girlfriend that easily."

Faith burst out laughing.

Lance frowned at her before turning back to Keira. "This isn't a laughing matter."

"I'm not the one laughing."

"Sorry," Faith called out. "I'll stop." She chuckled again, then grinned.

Asher smiled at his wife, then winked at Keira. "I agree that Lance shouldn't dump you so soon in your relationship." He arched a brow at Lance. "And you're not dumping your work family either. We're in this with you."

"Agreed," Faith added.

"When one of us is in trouble, we all are," Ryland said.

The others joined in, voicing their agreement. Every one of them.

"The time for debate is over," Ryland warned. "From now on, this case, your case, is the only one that Unfinished Business is working. And we're damn well going to solve it."

Lance hadn't been this frustrated, or touched, in a long time. Part of him wanted to shout at them to stop being so selfless, to just let him walk out the door. But the other part was so moved by their determination to help him that he was having difficulty forming words.

Keira seemed to sense his turmoil when she yet again took his hand in hers. "All for one and one for all. Is that the Unfinished Business motto?"

He cleared his throat, threading his fingers with hers. "Apparently so. Though I imagine the Three Musketeers might disagree."

Ryland stood. "We need to clear our schedules, make plans, hand out assignments. Lance, you'll have to go far more in-depth about OPI than the overview you just gave us. We need information on the cases you worked, dates, the names of anyone and everyone you had contact with while you worked there, no matter how unimportant it might seem. Let's get some coffee going and get comfortable. We'll likely be here most of the night. And many more after that."

Lance held up a hand to stop everyone. "One more thing, not that we need any added stress at this point. We don't think any other gunmen were still alive after this morning's attack, but we should all consider that someone may have remained in the woods watching. They could be watching all of us now, maybe even outside of this building. Everyone needs to be hypervigilant about your safety, and your loved ones' safety, until this is over."

Chapter Seven

Keira yawned in the back seat of UB investigator Adam Trent's truck, keeping her gaze averted from the steep drops down the side of the mountain road as they bumped along in the dark. Lance was in the passenger seat in front of her, talking to Trent. The night had been much longer than any of them had expected. Sunrise was only minutes away. And none of them had gotten any sleep yet.

Turned out, Grayson and Willow's influence with Police Chief Russo hadn't gone as they'd hoped. Eight dead bodies was just too much to explain away without a proper investigation. Russo had insisted on interviewing everyone again who'd been at the cabin and wouldn't back down. The only concession he made was to conduct the interviews at Unfinished Business because of Grayson's insistence on wanting to keep his team out of the media spotlight.

The interviews had gone well, considering. The roughest part for Keira was trying to pretend that she and Lance were a couple. Not knowing exactly what he was saying about her in his interview, she'd vaguely glossed over their relationship details and kept her answers brief. They must have both satisfied the detectives, because they were told they could go.

After a seemingly endless trip along winding narrow

roads they finally turned onto a relatively straight and flat one. The sun's first rays revealed that they were in a valley. The Smokies formed a misty white backdrop to a sparkling pond with a fountain in the middle. White three-rail wooden fences lined the road, only falling away when the truck turned once more and approached an ultramodern take on a traditional farmhouse.

Two stories of black siding were trimmed in crisp white. Charcoal-gray stone framed the bottom of the home. And a slate chimney rose up the left end. Instead of a wrap-around porch, there was a stone-wrapped portico in front, held up by thick cedar posts. A three-car garage flanked the large house on the right side.

This was Lance's home, the horse ranch he'd told her about when he'd arranged for them to get a ride with Trent. They certainly couldn't return to her rental cabin. And both of their vehicles had been shot up and were still being held as part of the ongoing crime scene investigation.

Lance had assured her and Trent that it would be safe to go to his home for a short time. The property deed wasn't registered under his name. It was listed under a tangle of shell companies that would take someone a long time to unravel. Still, they didn't plan on staying. He was retrieving his OPI files for Trent to take back to UB. And he had another vehicle in the garage for him and Keira to use.

Packing a suitcase was another item he'd said was on his to-do list, along with arranging for the care of his handful of horses while he and Keira left town. For her part, she already had her suitcase. That was yet another concession made by Chief Russo. He'd had a police woman pack her things at the rental cabin and take it to Unfinished Business for her.

"Do you prefer to wait in the truck?"

She blinked and realized that Lance was standing beside the truck, holding her door open.

"Oh, sorry. Was just...admiring your house. It's beautiful."

He smiled. "It's home. Wish we had more time and I could give you the grand tour. You're welcome to explore inside on your own while I get what I need."

"I just might." She hopped out of the truck, and the three of them headed inside.

Just like the outside, the interior of the house was a study in masculinity, blacks and browns with lots of dark stone accents. The ceilings were unusually high on the first level for a two-story home. She wouldn't have even realized there was a second level if she hadn't known from the outside. This open, expansive house was something she could breathe in. Her discomfort with tight spaces wouldn't be a problem here at all.

Lance motioned toward a massive cedar-and-granite island on the left side of the room. "Help yourself to something to eat if you're hungry. Otherwise, we can grab breakfast on our way out of town."

She would have thanked him, but he and Trent had already turned away and were heading toward a door on the far right side of the room, presumably to Lance's office. She heard their deep voices in conversation as they disappeared inside. With all the stress of the long day and night behind her, she was more inclined to want to sleep than eat. But if she lay down on one of the two groupings of black leather couches, she'd probably never get back up. They looked far too comfortable for her weary body. Instead, she meandered around, learning about Lance from the way this bachelor had chosen to furnish and decorate his home.

Dark colors were definitely his thing. There were no pinks or pastels, no feminine touches anywhere, except perhaps for a few pillows and blankets thrown over a chair and one of the couches. But she imagined those were more for comfort and warmth than to soften up the place.

He was a reader, something they both had in common. She practically drooled over the chunky floor-to-ceiling bookshelves she could see through an archway by the kitchen area. A ladder attached to a brass rail declared it to be his home library. And as she got closer, she could see there was nothing techie to interfere with the ambience. There were only books here, comfortable reading chairs and a gas fireplace on one end. She would have preferred the coziness of a wood-burning fireplace. But she could see the advantage of gas in this particular room. There wouldn't be any concern about smoke or soot damaging the books.

Part of her wanted to check the rest of this gorgeous house out, give herself that grand tour. But the reader in her couldn't pull herself away from this room. She scanned the bookshelves, delighted and in awe of his collection. There was one whole section of classics, many leather bound. Several appeared to be first editions. But she didn't want to risk damaging them by touching them, so she couldn't be sure.

Other shelves held all kinds of nonfiction, with a heavy emphasis on autobiographies and biographies of people all throughout history. Those were the most worn books, reflecting his love of knowledge rather than a desire to lose himself in a good story. Her preference was fiction, tales of every kind, from thrillers to fantasy, and her personal favorite, historical romance. Unfortunately, she didn't find any romance on his shelves. But there was a thick fantasy novel she'd love to sink her literary teeth into. Perhaps it wouldn't be too much to ask to borrow it.

The pleasing timbre of male voices again had her turning around, clasping the novel to her chest. Trent and Lance stood at the end of the foyer talking. Two large boxes were on the floor beside them, presumably the promised OPI files.

She headed over, relieved to see Lance smile at her holding the book, nodding as if to let her know he approved of her choice. She waited beside him as Trent summarized the plans they'd made earlier, as if to double-check that they were all on the same page.

"Asher and Faith are tasked with finding former OPI team member Melissa Temple. Ivy and I will search for Sam McIntosh. Callum and Brice are in charge of locating Jack Scanlon. You and Keira will look for Brett Foster. That leaves…" He thumbed through some texts on his phone.

"Mick Thompson," Lance told him.

"Right. Thompson. As soon as one of the teams I just mentioned frees up, they'll look for him. Grayson, Willow, Ryland and our TBI liaison, Rowan, will provide support from UB for all of us. They'll also run interference with Chief Russo. And they'll get started right away on these OPI files to help us locate your former teammates and to take a fresh look at what happened. Hopefully they'll find a thread to pull, something that will lead us to the mole sooner than later. Sound good?"

"Sounds real good. Thanks, Trent."

Trent responded by clasping Lance on the shoulder and nodding at Keira. "Both of you, please, keep in contact. If anything concerning pops up, let us know. We'll do the same."

Keira smiled her agreement.

Lance motioned toward the boxes. "Let me help you with those."

They each carried a box out to Trent's truck. When Trent was driving away, Lance rejoined Keira in the main room. He motioned toward the book in her hand. "One of my favorite epic fantasies. You read Rebecca Yarros?"

"Not yet. I've heard great things about this book and have been wanting to try it. Do you mind?"

"Of course not. Although I don't know how much reading time we'll get in the next few days, or however long this takes. If nothing else, you can take it back to Maple Falls once we've secured your safety and ability to return." He gave her an apologetic look. "I really am sorry you've been caught up in all this."

On impulse, she set the book on an end table and took one of his hands in both of hers. The warmth of his skin sent a shiver of delight up her spine and had her face flushing hot, especially when his eyes widened in surprise. But he didn't pull away, and she didn't let go.

"I don't think I've ever heard a man apologize as much as you have to everyone over the past—what?—twenty-four hours? I wish you'd stop. None of this is your fault. Seems to me that you've spent the past decade, even longer, fighting just to stay alive while keeping track of your team to try to keep them safe too. You didn't choose this path. But you darn well have the integrity to see it through and protect others, including me. That's not something to apologize for or feel bad about. It's admirable, honorable. Can we stop with the apologies?"

Ever so slowly, he lifted his other hand toward her face as if to give her time to stop him.

She didn't.

He feathered his fingers lightly across her cheek, then through her hair, gently pushing it back before dropping his hand. "You're something else, you know that?"

She drew a shaky breath, more affected by that light touch than she could have imagined. "Is being 'something else' good or bad?"

His lips curved in a sexy smile that had her hot and cold all over. Mostly hot.

"Definitely good," he said. "Maybe after this is all… resolved, I should take my chances about asking you out."

"Maybe you should."

He grinned. "Don't think for a second I'll forget you said that."

She would have made another sassy retort, but her brain cells seemed to have drowned in the rush of hormones flooding her system.

"Keira?" His deep tone was laced with humor.

"Um, yes?"

"I need to check on the horses before we leave."

"Right. Okay."

He glanced down at his other hand tightly clutched in hers.

"Oh!" She immediately let go, her face flushing hot. "Sorry."

He leaned down and pressed the lightest, barest kiss against her cheek, then winked. "I'm not. Wait here and I'll just step out back—"

"No. I'm going with you."

At his raised brows, her face flushed again. "I'd rather go with you to back you up if something happens." She tapped the holster concealed beneath her jacket, where she had her pistol. "Cop. Remember?"

"I remember. I used to be one too, you know."

"For eight years. In Nashville. Heck of a coincidence."

"Coincidence?"

"Nashville. My hometown."

"Right. Where your…complicated family lives, I assume?"

She stiffened. "Out back you said? That door off the kitchen?"

His smile widened. "Your excellent detecting skills are showing again." He held out his hand. "Come on. I'll show you my horses."

"That pickup line needs work," she teased, ignoring his hand as she headed toward the back door.

He chuckled and followed behind. Once outside, however, his amusement evaporated. Instead, he was fully alert, scanning the property and the outbuilding they were heading toward.

Feeling silly for flirting with him when both their lives were potentially in danger, she went on high alert too, in full police mode. She kept her right hand down near the holster she'd donned from her suitcase earlier and scanned for any hint of trouble.

When they reached the building, she expected him to pull out a key to unlock the doors to the stables. Instead, there was an electronic keypad beside it. But he didn't press the buttons. He pressed his hand against a black square beneath it. The doors clicked and a barely audible motor hummed, making the doors slide open.

Inside was no less modern and masculine than his house had been. Black metal rafters supported the roof instead of wooden beams. Pristine stone floors that gently sloped to rectangular drains on either side of the aisle no doubt made cleaning much easier than the dirt floors she'd expected. Sturdy cedar formed the stalls on either side.

"There are only four horses here right now," he said as she followed him down the aisle. "But it can hold up to eight. I figure one day, if I'm lucky enough to turn old and gray and still have this place, I'll fill the other stalls with little fillies and colts for my children and grandchildren."

"That sounds wonderful," she breathed, picturing it in her mind.

He stopped and looked at her over his shoulder. "You like horses?"

She laughed. "Honestly, I don't know. I've never seen one up close. Our family couldn't afford things like that when I was growing up."

He slowly nodded. "I forget sometimes just how blessed I am. We always had horses. Now I suppose I'm carrying on the family tradition. I just wish my dad could see this place."

She looked up at him, the sadness in his voice making her throat tight. "Maybe when this is over, when we stop the person behind what happened at OPI, you can see him again."

His jaw tightened, but he didn't say anything.

She stopped at the next stall, shaking her head in wonder at the beautiful animal poking its graceful head over the top of the stall door. "I can't imagine any father not approving of this. The house, the land, this place and, oh my goodness, these beautiful babies. They're amazing." She laughed when the reddish-brown horse closest to her snuffled at her shirt.

When she reached up to touch its muzzle, Lance grabbed her hand.

"Careful," he said. "She's looking for something to eat. I'd rather you kept your fingers."

Keira blinked and took a quick step back.

"I didn't mean to scare you. She's not mean. But she might bite on accident if you stick your fingers out like that. Here." He opened a metal bin in the wall behind her and pulled out a carrot. "Do it like this. Flatten your palm."

He broke the carrot in half and put one piece on his palm and held it up toward the horse. She snuffled his hand, grasping the carrot and pulling it into her mouth.

"Want to try?" He handed Keira the other half of the carrot.

"Definitely." She did what he'd shown her, laughing when the horse's velvety lips tickled her hand and took the carrot. "Oh my goodness. She's so sweet. And so very beautiful."

His dark eyes captured hers as he responded. "She most definitely is."

The wink that followed told her he definitely wasn't talking about the horse. She tried to respond and again couldn't seem to find her voice.

He took mercy on her, taking her hand in his. "Come on. We need to hurry. I don't think anyone will figure out about this place. But I'd rather not risk it. I need to get something from this last stall over here, the empty one on the left."

When they reached the stall, he let her hand go and crossed to the far wall.

"You mentioned the horses were hungry. Should I feed them?" she asked.

"If we had time, I'd love to show you how to do exactly that. They need oats, fresh hay, water. The carrots are treats, not a meal. I called a friend from my home office earlier to take care of that. He'll be here soon to get them." He reached above his head toward a piece of cedar trim.

"Get them? He's taking the horses away?"

Lance half turned, all serious again without a hint of his earlier lightheartedness. "If the wrong people figure out this is my place, I don't expect it to be standing when I return. The horses will be at my neighbor's stable, someone I trust." He turned back to the wall.

The idea that someone would destroy his beautiful home and this stable brought tears to her eyes. But whatever she might have been about to say was forgotten when the back stall wall slid open to reveal a narrow hidden room.

He headed inside, and by the time she followed, lights had flipped on, and he was pressing on another panel. It too slid open, but instead of another room, it revealed a metal safe built into the wall. There was a small desk and chair beside it, but nothing else. He crouched in front of the safe.

"Lance? What is this place? What are we doing here?"

"Saving my team. Hopefully."

"Saving your…which one? OPI? Or UB?"

He glanced back at her. "Both." He quickly pressed a sequence of buttons. The door on the safe popped open. A small leather duffel bag sat on the bottom shelf. Above it was a dark brown accordion folder about three inches thick.

"Lance, please. What are you…?" Again she stopped, this time in shock. He'd pulled out the duffel bag and opened it on top of the desk. Even from a few feet away, she could easily see what was inside.

Money.

A *lot* of money, bills of various denominations banded together.

"My goodness. That has to be thousands of dollars."

"It's enough."

"Enough for what?"

"To ensure our safety." After double-checking the contents, he zipped it closed and set it onto the floor. "We can't use credit cards, ATMs, anything traceable. We'll pay for everything we need in cash. I've also got IDs in the bag under various aliases, extra pistols and magazines of ammunition."

"I've heard of people having go bags to grab in an emergency, but normally they have clothes and toiletry items in them."

"I always figured I could buy those things wherever I ended up, if I didn't have a chance to pack a suitcase of clothes before I left. ID, cash, weapons—those are harder to get when traveling."

"Makes sense, I suppose. I've never felt the need for a go bag. Until now. I wish I'd packed extra ammunition before coming here."

"You've got a nine-mil right?"

She nodded, patting her jacket, hiding the bulge of her holster. "A Glock seventeen."

"My primary weapon is a Sig Sauer P320, nine millimeter. We can share ammunition. I'll pack extra."

"Thanks. I'll pay you back if we end up needing that ammo."

"Let's hope we don't." He sat at the desk. It barely surprised her this time when he slid more panels back and suddenly had a computer monitor in front of him with a keyboard on top of the desk.

She stepped to his side, glancing down at the bag of money, IDs and weaponry. "Lance. It's fine for you to use your money for your own protection. But I don't want you using it for mine. It had to have taken you years to save all that. We can make one stop at a local bank, and I can pull out my savings."

He'd been typing on the keyboard but stopped and looked at her. "It didn't take any time at all. I had terrible judgment when I first started out in joining OPI. But the one thing it did was give me more money than I could ever spend. And Grayson Prescott, my current boss? He's a billionaire, Keira. He pays us enough that we'll never have to worry about financial security. So don't worry about using that cash. There's plenty more."

She swallowed, then nodded. "Thank you. For helping to protect me. You're exceedingly generous with your money, your time. I just hope it doesn't end up costing you your life." She motioned to the room around them, the safe, the computer. "For you to have gone to all this trouble, the people we're up against must be far more dangerous than I'd even suspected."

"They're dangerous, yes. But only because they hide in the shadows. The mole, even with all the resources at his disposal, is still just a person, Keira. He's not superhuman, no more powerful than anyone else. All we have to do is bring him out of those shadows and into the light. We're going to survive this. Together. Trust me. And trust yourself. I've seen your courage. You ran out of the cabin when you could have stayed inside and been safe. But you didn't. You ran outside thinking I needed help."

She rolled her eyes. "Fat lot of good I did. You didn't need help. I did. I almost got you killed."

Again her hand somehow found its way into his. He threaded their fingers together, his large, strong hand engulfing hers, but gentle. So gentle her heart seemed to shift in her chest.

"You ran toward possible danger, Keira. For me. You

didn't know what or who might be out there. You still went outside. You're a good cop and a good person. And stronger than you know. Rely on your training. Trust yourself."

She offered him a tremulous smile. "Whatever happens, don't forget to ask me out on that date, okay?"

He pulled her hand to his mouth and kissed the back of it, just like the heroes in those historical romance novels she loved to read.

"I won't forget," he whispered against her hand, his warm breath making her shiver. He gently squeezed, then let go. "Just one more thing before we leave."

She pressed her hands together, covering the warm spot where his mouth had been. But the warm feelings flooding through her began to cool and freeze as she saw what he was doing. And began to understand.

The first call he placed through the computer was to someone the computer screen listed as Melissa. As soon as a voice answered, the computer voice spoke. "It was the best of times, it was the worst of times."

The call ended.

Lance pressed a few buttons and a second call went out. To Sam.

The computer announced the same phrase. "It was the best of times, it was the worst of times."

Another call. This one to Mick. The next was to Jack. Then, finally, Brett.

After Lance made the computer disappear and closed the wall over the safe, he straightened and stood directly in front of her.

She didn't meet his gaze.

His hand gently but firmly pressed her chin up until she was looking at him, his gaze locked with hers. "Ask me," he said. "Say it."

She stared at him for a long moment. Finally she said, "I'm surprised you chose Charles Dickens as your safe phrase to warn your old team."

He stared at her for an equally long moment. "What would you have chosen?"

She clenched her fists at her sides. "Nothing at all. Because I wouldn't have lied to my current team. I wouldn't send the UB investigators on a useless mission to try to find the OPI team members when you've known all along where they are. You knew Rick was in Maple Falls too, didn't you? Before you answer, think very carefully. Because I'm mad as hell. Don't lie to me. Did you or did you not know that Rick Cameron was in Maple Falls coming here to see you?"

The skin along his jaw whitened. "Do you honestly think that if I knew my friend was in trouble that I wouldn't have gone to help him? That I'd just let him die?"

She leaned toward him. "Isn't that what you're doing right now? Or at least risking the lives of your current friends when there's no reason to risk them at all? You can simply pick up the phone and call Trent, call the others and tell them there's no need to look for anyone. What kind of game are you playing?"

He swore, then scrubbed his face with his hands. "This isn't a game. You think I'm risking my UB friends' lives by sending them on a wild-goose chase? Just the opposite. The information in those files that I gave Trent is ancient history. It won't lead them to danger. It will keep them away while I take care of this damned mole once and for all."

She stared at him, blinking in surprise. "What the…? Everything you told them was a lie?"

He arched a brow. "Actually, my very first statement

was the truth, that everything they know about me is a lie. I just continued the charade. Not because I'm some sadistic jerk but because I care about them. They're married, have girlfriends, families. Grayson has a little girl from his first wife who was murdered. He only recently found her after she'd been missing for years. I don't want to be the reason she loses her father after only just meeting him.

"Today, with everyone confronting me, I was trapped. Trapped by my own team trying to force me to involve them in my own mistakes. Well, that's not going to happen. When I left UB this morning, heck, yesterday morning now, to go see you, I wasn't going to return. Ever. If things don't go the way I hope they do, that will still be my plan."

"Wow. I can't believe this. Did you not hear anything they said? It makes sense for them to help you. To help us. What makes you think that you can fight this mole on your own when you haven't been able to figure out who he is in over a decade?"

His jaw worked again. "Do you honestly think I haven't been searching for the mole ever since I left OPI? He forced me to give up my own family, forced all of us to do that, to keep them safe. I'm close, Keira. I've got all kinds of information, evidence, showing this mole's movements over the years. His electronic trail. And I've eliminated dozens of people through my investigation."

He let out a deep breath. "There are only a handful of people left who could be the mole, people who were in a position of power back when we were at OPI. People who hid behind the scenes and who I've discovered and focused on. I'm ready to end this, once and for all. I just need to find that one crumb, that one more piece of the puzzle that makes the whole picture come into focus. Then I can bring him to justice. I can end this."

She stared at him, stunned. "You think you're close to solving it?"

"I know I am. The death of Levi was a huge clue. Something he did put the mole on his trail. But I didn't take it as a clue or realize the significance until you came here and told me that Rick had been murdered. Their deaths, so close together, can't be a coincidence. All I have to do is find the link between them. That will be the key to narrowing my list of suspects down to one."

"That's a lot of speculation and uncertainty to be betting our lives on being able to take this mole down without help from Unfinished Business. Are you forgetting what happened at my cabin? We were almost killed."

"Don't you think I know that? It's all I can think about, how close you came to being killed."

She stared at him in surprise, then cleared her throat. "Okay. Then it's clear that I should have a say in this too. My fate is tied up in the results of this new search, finding this guy and stopping him. Because of that, I get input into what we do. And I want UB working with us. I don't think we can win this without them."

He stared at her a long moment, then swore beneath his breath. "I'm not going to change your mind on this, am I?"

"No."

"Good to know. If you're scared and don't have confidence that we can handle this on our own, then you shouldn't come with me."

"I shouldn't…wait. No. That's not what I meant."

A thumping noise sounded from somewhere inside the stables. "Lance? I'm here, like you asked. Where are you?"

Keira frowned and looked over her shoulder.

"In here," Lance called out. "Last stall on the left."

There was a sudden yank at her waist, and then something cold snapped around her left wrist. She whirled around, shocked to see Lance tossing her pistol onto the desk. He must have grabbed it from her holster. And there was a silver circle of metal shining around her wrist.

"Handcuffs? What the…?" Lance tugged her forward and snapped the other cuff around a metal ring on the wall that she hadn't noticed earlier. "What are you doing? Take these off."

A tall, imposing-looking man in his mid to late forties peered in through the opening, seemingly unsurprised to find the secret room. But his eyebrows rose when he saw Keira with her arm cuffed to the wall. "Hey, Lance. If you two are in the middle of something kinky, I can come back later."

"Shut up, Duncan."

Duncan laughed.

Keira rattled the cuffs. "This isn't funny. Lance, take these off."

"Duncan, can you give us a minute?"

"I can give you a whole lot of minutes while I load the horses. I'll come back after." He disappeared back into the stables.

Keira yanked on the cuffs again.

Lance swore and grabbed her arm. "Stop. You're going to hurt yourself."

"*You're* hurting me. You did this. You're responsible. Take them off now and I won't press charges."

He sighed heavily and let her go. "I'm sorry about this. I really am. I'll have Duncan take those off as soon as I'm gone. Have him take you to Unfinished Business. You can tell everyone the truth. It won't matter once I leave. They won't know where I'm going."

He turned away.

"Wait," she called out, panic making her voice shake.

"What now?"

"Please. Please let me go with you. I can help. I'll watch your back."

"No." He started to turn away again.

"Lance!"

His answering sigh could have knocked over one of the cypress timbers on the other side of the door. "One more question," he said, "then I'm out of here."

She licked her dry lips. "Why are you doing this? Why are you cutting me out of the investigation? It's not just about UB, keeping them out of it. There has to be more to it. You don't actually believe what you said earlier, about me being smart or courageous or that I could be an asset in your search. You think what, that I'd be a hindrance?"

His gaze locked on hers, and he was suddenly standing right in front of her. "I never lied about my belief in your abilities, Keira." He slowly shook his head as he stared down at her. "You're just as smart and courageous as I said, probably more. And you would definitely be an asset in any investigation."

"Then why? Why don't you want me to go with you?"

He flattened the palms of his hands on the wall on either side of her, his body so close they were almost touching. "I was going to. But when you were so adamant about not wanting to do this without my UB team, it made me rethink why I'd involve you when the whole reason I'm not involving them is to protect them. God knows I don't want anything bad to happen to you either. So why risk it? As impossible as it sounds, you're the best thing that's happened to me in a long time. We barely know each other, but I know this. I *want* to know you, learn everything about you. I want to take you out on a date, two dates, a dozen. But most of all, I want—I need for you to be safe."

Her whole body seemed to catch fire with his words. "Lance, are…are you saying you want to be my boyfriend?"

He choked on his laughter, coughed, then grinned. "Yeah. I guess that's what I'm saying."

"Prove it. Kiss me."

The sound of horses' hooves clopping through the stables had him stepping back. "I have to—"

"Lance. *Kiss* me."

His eyes darkened to a stormy blue. His gaze dipped to her mouth.

She closed the short distance between them, her breasts crushed against his chest as she angled her lips up toward his. "Lance?"

"I'm going to hell for this."

"Worth it."

He groaned deep in his throat. Then she was in his arms, and his mouth was doing all kinds of incredible things to hers. Good grief, this man could kiss. She wanted to wrap herself around him and hold on and never let go, give him back as good as he was giving her. And at first, she allowed herself to respond, to enjoy. After all, a piece of heaven was being dangled in front of her. And she was too weak not to take it. But as amazing as being in his arms felt, the awkwardness of her left arm being cuffed to the wall was enough to help her keep her wits about her and remember why she'd initiated this embrace in the first place.

She suddenly twisted against him and yanked his pistol out of his holster.

His eyes flew open as she pressed the gun's muzzle against his flat belly.

Ever so slowly, he pulled back and looked down between them at his gun, and her finger on the trigger.

"You've got two choices, Lance."

He slowly raised his head and waited.

"You can unlock these handcuffs and promise that you'll take me with you to find the mole."

His jaw worked, anger darkening his eyes even more. "Or?"

She shoved the gun against him. "Or you can bet your life that you know me well enough, after only a day, to be sure that a trained police officer isn't going to shoot a man who kidnapped her and chained her to a wall."

Their standoff went on for nearly a minute. Finally, Lance pulled the handcuff keys out of his pocket.

Chapter Eight

"You wouldn't really have shot me, would you?"

Keira sat beside Lance in the dark blue SUV he'd had in his garage, once again bumping down mountain roads. But this time, thankfully, they were heading out of Gatlinburg. Soon they'd be on wider, safer roads without the constant drop-offs beside them.

"I guess we'll never know for sure," she said.

He frowned and glanced at her, then focused on the road in front of them. "Regardless, you earned the right to be a part of this hunt for the mole. But once this is done, we're done. Before we ever got a chance to get started."

His words caused an ache in her chest that was hard to hide. But she did her best to pretend they didn't bother her. "You really know how to hold a grudge."

"A grudge? You had your finger on the trigger, not the gun frame. The trigger."

"I had to. Otherwise you'd have made some kind of move, tried to grab the gun away from me."

He glanced at her again. "Fair enough. Still, your finger could have accidentally jerked or squeezed just enough on that trigger to kill me even without meaning to. That's not something I'll forget."

"I guess that first date is no longer on the table then."

"We both know the answer to that."

She smiled, but inside she was raw, hurt, tired and so angry she wanted to hit something. To shatter some glass. Bust a chair into little pieces like they did in those action movies. All she'd wanted when she came here was to get justice for a murdered man. And now her entire world had been yanked out from under her. This…thing, this bond or whatever the two of them felt for each other, shouldn't even matter with everything else that was going on. But, dang it, it did. And every time he looked at her in derision or anger or said something like he'd just said, it was another dagger to her heart.

It would be comical if it wasn't so painful. In spite of all those romance novels she enjoyed, she didn't believe in instant love. But she did believe in instant connections, in feeling powerfully drawn to someone even before knowing them all that well. After all, she'd felt that with Lance. She *still* felt that way in spite of her heart being battered and bruised. And the hopeless romantic in her would probably always wonder *What if?* when it came to Lance Cabrera.

LANCE'S GRIP RELAXED on the steering wheel at the sound of Keira's deep, even breathing. She'd fallen asleep against the passenger door, looking as miserable as he felt.

How had everything gone so wrong?

All he'd wanted was to protect the people in his life who'd had no part of his bad decisions at OPI. They were innocent, both his friends at UB and Keira. It wasn't right to drag any of them into the danger that he'd brought to their door. Instead, he'd likely alienated his UB family, once they found out he'd tricked them. And he'd certainly ended any chance he'd had with Keira.

Was he angry with her? Hell yes. But that anger was already beginning to fade, and regret was digging its talons into him. Could he have taken his pistol away from her without getting shot? Maybe. Probably. But he hadn't tried because of one element to the situation that she hadn't thought through.

Duncan.

He was one of the few people Lance trusted completely outside of Unfinished Business. He wasn't just a guy Lance hired when he needed someone to look after his animals. He was a close friend. If Keira had shot Lance, Duncan would have shot her. And that wasn't something Lance could risk. So he'd gone along with her threat, letting her believe it was only because he was concerned for himself, when he was more concerned for her. And rather than go back on his word to let her accompany him on the search for the mole, he'd stood by his promise.

Lying to her again and not letting her come with him wasn't something he could stomach. But he still would have, in a heartbeat, if he thought she'd be safer that way. However, having seen firsthand how obsessed she was with finding the mole, he'd finally realized that nothing was going to keep her from pursuing this. It made more sense to keep her with him so he could look after her than to constantly wonder when and where she'd show up. He couldn't bear being the cause of her getting hurt, or worse. So the lesser of two evils seemed to be to keep his word and treat her as his partner in this hunt.

As for this crazy obsession he had for her, well, he'd just have to get over it. There was no way she'd ever forgive him for what he'd done. And he wasn't sure he could forgive her either. She could so easily have killed him. All because he'd cared enough to try to protect her. That whole stupid incident had destroyed their trust in each other. Without trust, a relationship was impossible.

He silently swore. He hadn't been this mixed up in the head since Ileana. She'd twisted him inside and out, leaving him, coming back, over and over until he didn't know what he felt anymore. With her out of his life once and for all, he'd finally been on an even keel again. And now here he was letting another woman tilt his world. Not in a good way either.

Maybe the disaster at the stable was fate's way of waking him up, of keeping him from potentially making another mistake. But he hated that it had taken well over a decade for him to finally meet someone he could immediately see himself with long-term. And then for all of that to come crashing down.

Sleep deprivation. That's what all of this had to be. He wasn't normally this quick to anger, this confused. He'd matured since his days of being so easily manipulated by his ex. Now he approached life with logic, not his hormones. All he needed was a good night's sleep. He'd been up for well over twenty-four hours now. Heck, it was edging closer to thirty.

Lucky for both of them, the next exit had a decent hotel with a vacancy—a two-bedroom suite with two king-size beds. And the cash bribe he gave the night clerk was enough to get her to look past the fact that he didn't have a credit card to secure the room. His false ID and a wad of cash was all she'd needed in order to hand over the room key.

A bleary-eyed, exhausted Keira mumbled good-night without meeting his gaze, then clicked her bedroom door shut with him still standing in front of it.

His shoulders slumped in defeat. He so wished that he

could have a complete redo of the past day and a half. But life didn't come with a rewind button. And as he'd told his team earlier, some things couldn't be fixed.

Chapter Nine

When Keira stepped out of the hotel bedroom, freshly showered, in clean clothes and wearing enough makeup to hide the dark circles under her eyes, she stopped in surprise. The kitchenette had a pot of coffee made with a mug and packets of sweeteners beside it. Next to that was a box of delicious-looking breakfast pastries in varying types from apple to cinnamon to cream cheese and a handful of others. And just in case that wasn't what she fancied, there was a large bowl of sliced fruit and a loaf of bread sitting beside the toaster. But Lance was nowhere to be found.

His bedroom door was open, the bed visible through the doorway neatly made. The folder he'd had in his safe yesterday was open on the coffee table in front of the couch. Papers and pictures were spread out as if he'd been studying them earlier this morning. But the suite itself was sadly empty.

A slight movement to her left had her turning. Through a slit in the curtains she could see a man in a dark leather jacket standing at the balcony railing, a cup of coffee in his hands as he looked out at the Smoky Mountains. Lance.

The guilt that had her tossing and turning last night rode her hard. It was an uncomfortable feeling, one she wasn't used to.

She fixed herself a cup of coffee. One packet of sugar, none of that fake sweetener for her. And some creamer she'd been unsurprised to find in the refrigerator. After all, he'd thought of everything else she might want or need.

After returning to the bedroom to put on her long jacket against the chilly fall air, she grabbed her mug of coffee and headed outside. When she stepped onto the balcony, Lance smiled. But it was a shadow of his usual ones.

"Morning," he said.

"Morning. I come unarmed."

He lifted the edge of his jacket to show his pistol holstered to the belt of his jeans. "Can't say the same."

She wanted to joke about that, to say something to cut the tension. But nothing clever came to mind, so she didn't try.

They stood silently beside each other for several minutes, sipping their respective cups of coffee and staring out at the beautiful vista in front of them. This time of year, the Smokies were dressed in fading golds and oranges. Not the full-on brilliant colors that would have attracted leaf peepers a month earlier. But still colorful enough to steal her breath.

In spite of all those winding, narrow, terrifying roads without guardrails all over these mountains, she couldn't deny how amazing and awe-inspiring it would be to see this kind of scenery out her windows every day. But she'd prefer to see it from a valley looking up at the mountains rather than actually driving through them.

As she watched, thin white clouds moved over the peaks, dressing them in mist and dipping down into the higher elevations. A few minutes later, the mist rose, revealing the peaks again. But shadows from other clouds passed across the sun, emphasizing the deep variations of color dancing up and down the slopes.

"It really is beautiful here," she murmured, mostly to herself.

He set his coffee mug on the railing. "I've lived in this area for over three years and have never tired of the scenery. It's ever-changing. One minute, you can see for miles. The next, the mist settles in and you can barely see anything. In the summer, it's every shade of green you can imagine. Once the last of these autumn leaves drop, it will be gray and barren-looking to the casual observer. But if you pay close attention, you'll see things you couldn't see before. Bald spots and clearings between groves of trees. Evergreens interspersed between the spindly, naked birch and oak."

When he went silent, she prodded, "And in the spring? What's it like then?"

He smiled, as if at something only he could see. "Everything comes to life. Wildflowers dot the ranges. Trees leaf out, fill out, new branches climbing toward the bright blue sky. Baby rabbits, squirrels and chipmunks can be spotted hiding in the bushes, climbing trees, chattering at you when you encroach on their domain. At sunset the deer come out, mothers watching over their spotted fawns. Bucks scratching their antlers on the trees. Black bears are all around these parts. Mostly they stay hidden, but that time of year they wake up hungry from hibernation and eat everything they can. You'll spot some in the mountains or in town trying to score an easy meal from a careless tourist who tosses out their food without realizing it will attract wildlife."

She was mesmerized by the emotion in his voice, the wonder in his expression.

"You really do love it here, don't you?"

His smile faded as he faced her, resting his hip against the railing. "How could I not?"

"Well, for one thing, there are those narrow death-defying curvy roads up and down the mountains. I don't see how anyone could love those."

His mouth quirked up at one corner. "Believe it or not, you get used to them, barely think about it once it's part of your daily routine."

"I suppose. But it's hard to imagine. If I lived here, I'd rather stay in a low-lying area with some gently rolling hills. The mountains could form a gorgeous backdrop, in the distance."

"Sounds like my ranch."

She blinked. "Exactly like your ranch. It's beautiful."

They were both quiet for a minute, then...

"I'm sorry—" he said.

"I'm sorry—" she said at the same time.

They both laughed.

She stepped closer and put her hand on his, which was resting on top of the railing. "I mean it, Lance. I'm so very sorry for yesterday. I was shocked, angry, when you put those handcuffs on me. Even more angry that you were going to leave to pursue this investigation without me when my fate is involved as much as yours. But that's no excuse for what I did. I never should have put my finger on that trigger. You're right, one shake of my hand and I could have shot you." She swallowed against her tight throat. "I could have killed you. I'm so, so sorry."

He looked down at her hand on his, then slowly turned it so that they were holding hands. "I appreciate that. I'm sorry too, more than you can imagine. We both made mistakes. But it was my poor decision that started it all. Truce?"

She tightened her grip. "Truce."

He studied her, seeming uncertain. But then, as if he couldn't help himself, he gently pulled her toward him. He cradled her against his chest, his arms around her, hugging her close. When a brisk breeze made her shiver, he opened his coat and wrapped it around both of them, forming a warm cocoon.

Like a weary traveler finally coming home, her body relaxed against his. It felt unbelievably right being in his arms. And, man oh man, did he smell good, a mixture of coffee, soap, leather and the clean outdoors. The hard planes of his sculpted body fit against her curves as if he'd been made for her. It seemed silly even thinking that way, as if she were writing one of those romance novels. But it was true. She could have stood there forever, held by him. And dang if she didn't want to. But the world intruded all too soon. His cell phone buzzed in his coat pocket.

He murmured an apology as he extricated himself and stepped back to check his phone. When he saw the number, he grimaced and took the call.

"Hey, Trent."

She watched in surprise as he held the phone slightly away from his ear. Even from a few feet away, she could hear Trent's raised voice. He definitely wasn't happy.

Lance pressed the phone back to his ear. "I know, I know. I shouldn't have—" He winced again, then shook his head at Keira, his mouth quirking in that half grin she was beginning to become so familiar with.

"That's not going to happen." He sighed heavily as he listened to Trent's response. He stepped to the end of the balcony, leaning back against it, speaking on occasion but not really saying much.

When the call ended, he held the phone in his hand rather than slide it into his jacket pocket. "That was fun."

"What happened?" she asked. "He sounded angry."

"Yeah, well, he wasn't happy when Duncan told him I'd contacted my old team already and he and the others didn't need to try to find them."

She drew in a surprised breath. "You had Duncan tell them the truth?"

"Someone I know made me feel guilty." He winked. "At least now everything's in the open. He wants us to come back so we can work on this together since there's no reason to go searching for my old team now."

"Is that what we're doing? Going back?"

"We? No. But if you've changed your mind and don't want to go with me, I can have Duncan pick you up here and take you to UB."

"We haven't spoken about your plan. I'm guessing you're heading to New York City to look into Levi's death." She winced. "Long drive but I guess there's no other option or you wouldn't be able to bring your duffel full of weapons with you. From there, you'll try to find out whether Rick was there and whether it cost him his life too. At some point you'll head to Maple Falls to see the scene of the crime firsthand, the motel where Rick was murdered. Am I right?"

"I guess my answer depends on whether you've changed your mind about wanting to go with me. And yes, we'd be driving. Shouldn't be too rough with two drivers to switch off."

"We're in this together. Nothing's changing my mind. And I'm fine helping with the driving."

He smiled. "All right then. Heading to Maple Falls isn't in the equation. It's likely too dangerous."

"You think the mole's people are still there, watching for one of us to show up?"

"It's what I'd do. Besides, you're a walking, talking treasure trove of information about that investigation. And your copy of the case file has the crime scene photographs. We can review those together. But the first order of business is to look into Levi's death, as you said. It makes sense with everything that's happened that his murder was the catalyst to stir things up again. I want to try to figure out why he was killed and what put a target on his back. But he wasn't killed in New York City. He was killed in a small town in upstate New York called Newtown. When I mentioned New York in the UB meeting, I purposely implied that it was NYC to keep my team away from the actual location where Levi was killed."

She gave him a doubtful look. "If you found Levi's mugging story on the internet, so can your UB friends."

"I'm sure they will. But it will take time. It was a small article in an obscure paper. It's not going to come up high on any internet search engines. By the time they figure out the location, I'll have finished my investigation there and moved on to the next step."

"The next step?"

His jaw tightened. "I'm going to end this."

A feeling of dread snaked up her spine. "What, exactly, does that mean?"

Rather than answer, he checked his watch. "Trent's had all of three minutes to trace my phone. Even jumping through hoops with the phone carrier, I imagine he can bribe or threaten someone into helping him rather quickly. We probably have another five minutes, at best, before he has our location. It should take the team a good forty-five minutes to reach this hotel. But I wouldn't put it past them to call in help from Chief Russo and send a police car over here to cut that response time. We'll have to pack our breakfast to go." He winked, then picked up his phone and hurtled it deep into the woods beyond the balcony.

Keira stared at the trees where his phone had disappeared. "I sure hope that was a burner phone."

"Unfortunately, no. It was my personal phone. From here on out, we use burners so that my well-intentioned UB friends can't trace us. I do have another smartphone under my alias. It's never been used. No one will have any history of it to find us, so it's safe for internet searches or whatever else we may need. There are cheap burner phones in my go bag too. Untraceable, only good for phone calls. I'm happy to share." He held out his hand. "I will of course reimburse you for your loss."

She stared at him. "Please tell me you're kidding."

"Afraid not."

She swore and handed him her phone, cringing as he sent it hurtling into the trees.

Chapter Ten

Keira sat on the foot of the second of two queen-size beds in her and Lance's second-floor room in the only bed-and-breakfast in Newtown, New York. Lance stood a short distance away peering out the window down at Main Street.

"What do you see out there?"

He dropped the frilly curtain back into place. "Questions without answers. We walked the whole length of that street and back in, what, ten minutes? Fifteen? Newtown is even smaller than I thought it would be. There's absolutely nothing here to attract someone like Levi."

"He wasn't a nature lover? Hiker? Antique store aficionado?"

He scoffed. "Not even close. He hated living in Ocala, Florida, during our OPI days. He complained that there were more horses per capita than people." He smiled. "He might have been right. He was only there because the financial company his father worked for had transferred the family there when Levi was still in high school. He craved excitement, neon lights, plays, opera—the finer things in life. He was only biding his time in horse country until he felt he had enough money to quit and move somewhere like, well, New York City."

"Which is a good four hours from here," she said. "If he's a city-slicker type, why settle in Newtown?"

"That's what we need to find out."

"We should make a list of our to-do items," she said. "Divide and conquer. We can meet at the little café on the corner in a couple of hours and share what we've found."

He immediately shook his head no. "As small as this place is, I don't see any reason for us to split up. Without knowing whether the mole has people in town, watching for anyone asking about Levi's death, I'd rather not risk us each being on our own."

She shook her head in frustration. "You don't trust me to take care of myself. Still."

"Of course I do. I just don't see the need for it."

"The quicker we look into things here, the quicker we can move on to something else. Splitting up is the best way to do that."

He cocked his head. "Is it just me?"

"Just you…what?"

"That makes you defensive every time I suggest we do things a certain way."

"I'm not defensive. I'm just… I don't want to be coddled, that's all."

"Is it coddling to want to work together as partners, backing each other up rather than working separately?"

"Splitting up makes more sense," she insisted.

"No. It doesn't. It's far more dangerous, and you know it. So why are you getting your hackles up?"

She stiffened. "My *hackles*?"

"Poor choice of words. Come on, Keira. What is it? What am I doing wrong here?"

She blew out a deep breath, then shoved her hair back from her face. "Nothing."

He waited a moment. When she didn't say anything else, he asked, "Nothing meaning what exactly?"

"It's not you, okay? It's…men in general. The guys I work with in Maple Falls. The ones who ordered me around at my Nashville job. My father who…who…smothered me. Who wouldn't let me out of his sight. The man who… who…" She shook her head, squeezing her eyes shut. "It's not you. I'm sorry. It's just… I don't like being told what to do. Or protected. I don't… I don't—"

He sat beside her and pulled her onto his lap and into his arms. She stiffened, ready to push him away.

"Keira," he whispered against the top of her head. "Please, let me hold you. I'm asking. Not telling. I'm not coddling or protecting or telling you what to do. I'm here for you. You're in control. Please, let me be here for you. You're the one in control. It's okay."

You're the one in control.

And just like that, the floodgates opened. Instead of pushing his arms away, she held on tight, sobbing against his chest.

"It's okay," he whispered, his arms tightening around her. "It's okay. Let it out. You're in control."

His intuitive words had her sobbing harder, holding on to him so tightly it probably hurt. But she couldn't seem to let go or stop crying.

He rocked her back and forth, whispering over and over against the top of her head. "It's okay. It's okay. You're in control."

When she finally stopped crying and straightened, she gasped in embarrassment at his shirt. "I'm so sorry. Your shirt is soaked."

He smiled. "You can soak it any time you need to. I have other shirts."

She should have immediately gotten off his lap. But somehow, she couldn't seem to make herself even want to.

Instead, she stared into his eyes, just inches away. "How did you know that's what I needed to hear? I didn't even know I needed it."

Ever so gently, he feathered her hair back from her face. "Every time I make a decision for both of us, you push back. I thought maybe it was just me, that you didn't want to feel as if I was trying to force you into anything. But then, what you said…before you started crying… I realized it's not just me. It's something that happened to you, isn't it?"

She squeezed her eyes shut a moment, then let out a shaky breath. "Yes."

He waited. When she didn't say anything else, he asked, "Do you want to talk about it?"

For the first time in a very long time…no. For the first time *ever*, the idea of sharing what had happened instead of being forced to felt…right. As if she could somehow lighten the burden on her soul by sharing that burden with him. But when she opened her mouth to tell him, the words wouldn't come. She shook her head. "I…can't."

He gently kissed her forehead. "If you ever want to tell me, I'm here."

"Thank you," she whispered. "And… I really am sorry. For everything. You're right that I get prickly when someone tells me what to do. But I've been doing the same thing to you. I've been forcing you to let me come with you. That's not right either. I'm sorry, Lance. Truly."

He cocked his head. "You think you've been forcing me?"

"Well, yes. Like back in the stables, when I…" She squeezed her eyes shut for a moment. "When I made you promise, at gunpoint, to take me with you. That was wrong on so many levels."

"Kind of like me handcuffing you in the first place?"

She laughed. "Well, that was somewhat outrageous. I guess we both messed up."

"To a point."

She frowned. "What do you mean?"

He gently set her on her feet beside the bed and pulled out his pistol.

"Um, Lance? What are you doing?"

"Letting you know that you don't have to apologize." He dropped the magazine out of the pistol onto the bed, then ratcheted out the bullet in the chamber. Then he stood in front of her and handed the gun to her, pointing it at his belly just as she'd done back in the stables.

She swallowed and lowered the pistol. "Why are you doing this?"

"Trust me. It's not loaded, so it's safe. Hold the gun exactly as you did at my ranch."

When she hesitated, he said, "Please."

Hating what she was doing, and feeling worse than ever for having pointed it at him before, she held it in her right hand. Mimicking the way her left hand had been handcuffed to the wall, she raised her left arm.

"Now what?"

"Put your finger on the trigger."

"Lance, I don't…"

"Please."

She sighed heavily and did what he'd asked. "Okay, now—"

He moved with blinding speed. One moment the gun was in her hand. The next it was in his but aimed at the floor.

She blinked in shock, then looked up at him. "Oh my gosh. I never really had a chance, did I? At the stables."

He reloaded the pistol and holstered it at his waist. "I'd like to think not and that I could have taken it away just as easily. But there's always a possibility I couldn't have. Regardless, I think it's safe to say that you don't need to feel guilty for forcing me into anything I didn't want to do."

She nodded, humbled by his skills and reminded again that her few years in law enforcement didn't come close to his experience. "You need to teach me that trick sometime."

"After we bring the bad guy down, absolutely. Anytime. Maybe I'll show you how to ride a horse too, if you're game."

She smiled. "It's a date."

He grinned. "I knew I'd get you to say yes at some point."

"Overconfident," she chided.

"Highly motivated." He looked her up and down, then let out a slow sexy whistle.

She burst out laughing.

He laughed too, then crossed to the closet and pulled out a fresh shirt. She was about to tease him but whatever she was going to say flew out of her mind when he shrugged out of his wet shirt. His golden tanned skin rippled over his back muscles as he reached into the closet. His jeans hugged his narrow hips and cupped his perfectly proportioned backside. When he turned around, she had to bite back the low moan of desire that caught her by surprise. There wasn't an ounce of flab on his golden muscular abdomen. His chest and biceps would have made an artist weep at the chance to paint him. Heck, they made her want to weep with the urge to reach out and touch.

As he buttoned up and began tucking his shirt into his jeans, it did nothing to cover up the picture of him now firmly branded in her mind. How was she supposed to work with him now after having seen what was hiding underneath his clothes? Her gaze dipped to his jeans and her belly tightened.

He took some small photographs from his OPI folder and slid them into his shirt pocket. She took advantage of his inattention to hurry into the adjoining bathroom to compose herself.

"Let me fix my makeup and I'll be right out," she said as she closed the door.

"Take your time. Want me to wait downstairs?"

She blinked in horror at the dark tracks of mascara on her face from all her crying. "If you don't mind, that would be great."

"The key's on top of the dresser. I'll chat up the inn-keeper for any information I can get about Levi and Rick."

"Good idea."

At the sound of the door closing, she let out a pent-up breath. His reminder about his teammates had her want-ing to kick herself. She'd been on an emotional roller coaster, thinking about her past. That must have been why she'd gotten in such a dither over Lance's drool-worthy body. She shook her head. Yes, he was gorgeous. But that wasn't important right now. She had to focus on what really mattered.

Staying alive.

Chapter Eleven

Lance stood across the street from the police station thinking through possible scenarios of how he and Keira could get a copy of the case file and coroner's report on Levi's death.

Keira put her hands on her hips. "I can't imagine they'd tell me no after I explain that I'm in law enforcement. I've got my badge. I don't have to mention Rick's case. We can tell part of the truth—that Levi was a friend of yours and we'd like to find out more about what happened to him."

"The chief probably would let us look through the file. But we have to weigh the advantages versus the disadvantages. Although the innkeeper this morning didn't recognize Levi's picture when I showed it to him, he did recognize Rick's. So we've verified our theory that Rick was in town shortly after Levi's death notice was placed in the paper. We've already asked nearly every store owner on Main Street about Levi and Rick. The more we do that, the more we risk attracting the wrong kind of attention."

"You're not worried the mole will find out we're here, are you? We're registered at the B-and-B under your alias. Paying cash everywhere we go. Are you thinking the local police are in league with the mole and would tell him we're here in Newtown? That seems far-fetched."

"It does. But it also seems far-fetched that the mole would discover and murder two of my teammates a few months apart over a decade after we went on the run. Something has happened to stir things up. Without knowing what that was, we have to do everything we can to not broadcast our location. I'd rather find him before he finds us.

"To answer your question, though," he continued, "I have no reason to suspect the local police are involved in any of this. However, if you show your badge to the police chief, he's likely to want to call your boss to talk it out with him before providing access to the files. We already know the bad guys were in Maple Falls, that they followed you to Gatlinburg. They could still have the Maple Falls Police Station under surveillance. Maybe they've even got a wiretap to see if you check in with your boss. A call from here to your boss could be exactly what the mole needs to find us."

She shook her head. "Either you're ridiculously paranoid about this mole's reach and capabilities, or you're right and I need to get paranoid."

He smiled. "Maybe a little of both. We do have another option to get the files. It would be illegal. And risky."

She held her hands up. "We're not breaking into the police station or hacking into their computer system. I draw the line there."

"You wouldn't have to go with me. I could take care of it late at night when they have a skeleton staff. In and out."

"Are you serious?"

He sighed and scrubbed his jaw. "I'm serious that it's an option. I haven't made any decisions yet."

"You can't honestly believe that risking getting caught

and going to jail is better than me going the legal route and simply asking for a copy of the file."

He arched a brow. "I wouldn't get caught."

She rolled her eyes. "Someone needs to help you with this confidence problem of yours."

He laughed and checked the time on his phone. "I vote we grab an early dinner at the café and think all of this through."

"On that we can agree. Maybe that's why you're coming up with crazy ideas. We skipped lunch and your brain is running on empty."

He grinned. "Maybe that's it."

A few minutes later, they were sitting across from each other in a large booth at the back of the Corner Café. With it being between the traditional lunch and dinner hours, there weren't that many customers. And Lance had purposely asked to sit in that booth so he could have his back to the wall and keep an eye out for anyone coming close enough to overhear anything he and Keira talked about.

No sooner had their food arrived than the little bell over the entrance announced someone was coming in. Lance looked up, then swore.

Keira glanced at him in question, but before she could turn around, Trent and Asher were sliding into the booth beside them.

"What the hell are you doing here, Trent?" Lance demanded as Trent grabbed a french fry off his plate and set a file folder on the table. "And scoot over, Asher. You're crowding Keira."

Asher smiled at Keira and moved over. "Nice to see you again."

She slid closer to the wall, giving him more room. "Um, nice to see you too."

"No," Lance said. "It's not. What are you two doing here?"

Trent's shoulder brushed against him. Lance reluctantly moved over and shoved his plate with a cheeseburger and fries out of the way.

"Aren't you going to ask how we found you?" Trent asked.

"I'm sure it wasn't difficult. All you had to do was trace Levi to this town and then you called the only hotel here, gave them our descriptions, and the innkeeper ratted us out."

Asher laughed. "He totally did."

Lance shook his head. "I thought after I had Duncan give you the information I'd been accumulating about the mole and the people on my short list, you'd focus on that. Why interfere with Keira and me looking into my team member's deaths?"

Trent motioned toward Keira. "Knowing that the mole tracked Keira from Maple Falls to Gatlinburg suggests that he may still be watching for Keira and you. Which means you couldn't formally ask the police chief here in Newtown to give you the information that you need about Levi's death without risking having your names entered online and possibly triggering a notification to the mole." He tapped the folder. "So Asher and I got it for you."

Lance stared at him, afraid to hope. He flipped open the folder. Sure enough, the first few pages were the police reports about the mugging. After that were the hospital ER reports. And underneath that, even more notes on the investigation.

Trent motioned toward the folder. "That last group of pages is the coroner's report."

Lance started to pull that section out, then decided

against it. Levi was his friend. He wasn't mentally prepared to view autopsy photos and records of his injuries
just yet. He'd wait and review them later at the B-and-B.
He closed the folder. "I'm not sure what to say."

"You don't have to say anything." Trent clasped his
shoulder. "We told you that you and Keira aren't in this
alone. Whatever help you want or need from us, just let
us know. We respect your decision to work this angle by
yourselves. We'll continue looking into the higher-ups
in the agencies you pointed out in your research. When
you're ready to regroup and share information, let us
know."

Trent slid out of the booth and stood.

Asher did the same but paused to place another folder
on top of the first. "We're working in shifts at Unfinished
Business so that we've got someone moving your investigation forward at all hours. That's the summary of what
we've pulled together already. Of the five men you believe
could be the head bad guy, we've eliminated two of them."

Lance looked up in surprise. "You're sure?"

"Positive. At the time various events you pointed out
back at OPI transpired, those two wouldn't have had the
opportunity, or the power, to pull them off. The others
would. We're focusing on those remaining three now."

Asher nodded at Keira, who smiled back. She turned
the full wattage of her smile on Lance, who was still reel-
ing from everything that had just happened. When he was
finally able to break free from her beautiful smile, he realized his friends were almost to the door of the café. He
slid out of the booth and strode after them.

"Trent, Asher." They stopped at the door. Lance held
out his hand. "Thank you. I mean it. I've been an ass.
And it's taken me too dang long to realize it. I'll keep

you both posted on any progress that Keira and I make. Please thank the team for us."

Trent clasped his shoulder again. "We're only a phone call away, buddy." He stepped outside.

Asher shook Lance's hand, but his earlier amusement seemed to evaporate as he held on tight.

"You and I went through hell together when Faith was almost killed a few months ago. You were there for both of us. We're both here for you now. Don't forget that. And whatever you do, don't let your thirst for justice, or revenge, get you or Keira killed."

With that, he stepped out the door.

Lance watched as Trent and Asher crossed the street to Trent's car, more affected by Asher's words than he would have expected.

Don't let your thirst for justice, or revenge, get you or Keira killed.

"Lance? Everything okay?"

He turned at the sound of Keira's voice. *No. Nothing is okay.* He forced a smile and joined her at the table. "We can discuss the investigation later. Let's eat before our dinner gets cold."

"Late lunch, not dinner. Depending on how late we're up working, I may still require additional sustenance."

"I consider myself warned that I may have to raid the B-and-B kitchen at midnight."

"Count on it." She laughed and they sat down to their respective burgers and fries.

At the end of their meal, Lance picked up the folders to leave.

"Wait," she said. "At every place we've been today, we showed Levi and Rick's photographs. Might as well do that here too." She held out her hand. "I'll ask the staff. You can wait here."

He nodded his thanks and handed her the pictures from his shirt pocket.

A few minutes later, she returned and gave him back the photos. "No memories of Rick having been here. But Levi definitely ate here often. He was somewhat of a regular. One of the waitresses remembers him meeting a woman here maybe once a week."

"A woman. As in a friend?"

"More than friends, according to the waitress who remembers them best. Before you ask, no, she never heard their names. And since they paid in cash, there aren't any credit card receipts to look through. I asked her if she could describe the woman with Levi, and she said she was very pretty, with long dark hair and light brown skin. She was tall too, about the same height as Levi."

His stomach dropped, as if he'd just jumped off a cliff. "She's just shy of six feet tall then. A couple of inches shorter than me."

Keira's brow wrinkled with concern. "Lance? You don't sound right. What's going on now?"

"I need to ask the waitress something. Which one is she?"

"Alice, the same waitress who took our orders. The young blonde woman on the right by the drink machine."

He pulled out the smart burner phone that had internet capabilities and pulled up a picture. When he reached the waitress and tried to show her the picture, she kept smiling and blinking her obviously false eyelashes. It took several attempts to get the information he needed. And several more minutes to extricate himself from her groping hands without providing his phone number that she'd asked for.

Keira wasn't at their table anymore. Instead, she was standing by the door, watching through the glass as she clutched the folders against her chest.

"Thanks for getting the folders." Lance stopped beside her. "Ready?"

"That depends. Did you get what you wanted from that Dolly Parton wannabe?"

He blinked. "Our waitress? Alice?"

"Oh. Was that her name? I forgot." She pushed the door open and stepped outside.

He caught up to her and stopped her with a gentle hand on her shoulder. "Keira? Did I do something to upset you?"

She let out a deep breath, her cheeks flushing a light pink. "No. No, you didn't. I'm being…just forget it. Sorry. I'm not myself." She drew a steadying breath and he began to wonder if she could actually be jealous. Of groping Alice. The very idea was ludicrous. And interesting too if Keira was upset that Alice had been so clingy. Very interesting.

"Was Alice able to provide more information about Levi? Or his apparent girlfriend?"

He scrubbed his jaw, forcing himself to focus on the case. Not his attraction to the beautiful woman working the case with him.

"I showed her a picture from many years ago that my old roommate in college posted on our fraternity's website. It was a frat party. The picture was of me and some of my buddies with some women we were dating at the time. In spite of the years that have passed, Alice recognized one of the women in the photo as being the one she'd seen at the café. It was Ileana Sanchez."

Her eyes widened. "Your ex?"

He nodded, his throat tight. He still couldn't believe she'd turned up in the middle of this investigation.

"Yikes. How incredibly awkward for her to have dated your friend all these years later."

He slowly shook his head. "Ileana and Levi never would have dated. Levi Alexander was gay."

Chapter Twelve

Keira sat on her bed, thumbing through one of the stacks of papers that Trent and Asher had given them. On the other bed, Lance was doing the same.

She motioned toward the notes she'd been taking on a legal pad. "I've been thinking about Ileana and Levi acting lovey-dovey in the café. With him being gay, I can't figure out any reason for them to do that."

"The only one who can explain is Ileana."

"I'm guessing you have no clue where she lives these days, other than close to this place, in theory, if she was coming here on weekly visits."

"She wasn't part of OPI in any capacity. I had no reason to keep up with her after we all went underground. That might be something Trent and Asher can look into for us."

"You're going to take them up on their offer to help?"

He looked up from the page he was reading. "I've finally given in. I'm waving the white flag. I surrender to my team's good intentions in spite of my own intentions to keep them out of this."

She gave him a suspicious look. "And none of this sudden willingness for them to help has anything to do with you wanting to avoid your ex?"

He grinned. "It's a definite side benefit."

She laughed. "Want me to give Trent the good news?"

"If you don't mind. Take a burner phone. We'll only use it for contacting Trent. Make sure he knows that and not to pass the number around and only to call if or when absolutely necessary. We'll toss that phone in a couple of days."

As she got the burner from his duffel bag, she asked, "You don't really think the people looking for us would set up a massive trace for all of the UB investigators' phones do you?"

"No. I don't. But I'm still not willing to risk it." He told her Trent's number and she punched it in.

After she made the call, she went back to the reports on top of her comforter. The room went silent while they both read through the information they'd divvied up between the two of them. It was probably an hour later when she stiffly slid off the tall bed and stretched her aching back.

"I'm too young to feel this sore."

"We've been at this for hours. Take a break. Go downstairs and get that snack you talked about earlier."

"I remember you agreeing to pilfer from the kitchen when I'm ready for a snack. But you can relax. I'm not hungry yet. And I'm not ready for a break, not a long one at least. I just need to stretch and walk it off until I'm ready to bend over those papers again." She motioned toward his bed. "Find anything interesting yet? Any leads for us to follow?"

"Not much. Mainly I'm looking through the data that made UB conclude they could mark two people off my suspect list."

She stretched up toward the ceiling, then leaned over and touched her toes, her long hair falling over her face and sweeping the floor. When she straightened, and stretched toward the ceiling again, she asked, "Do you not agree with their conclusions?"

When he didn't respond, she lowered her arms and looked at him.

He was staring at her, his eyes darker than usual, tension in every line of his body.

"Lance? Is something wrong?"

He looked away, his jaw working. A moment later, he let out a long, deep breath. "Maybe we shouldn't have agreed to sleep in the same room."

She waited, but when he didn't say anything else, she asked, "Why not? There was only one room available. If we didn't stay here, we'd have had to drive an hour out of town to the next hotel."

She stretched again, trying to relieve the pressure in her shoulders.

"Keira?"

"Um?" She touched her toes again, reveling in how much better her back was starting to feel.

"That hotel might be safer."

She turned to face him, hands on her hips. "Safer? You think our location has been compromised?"

"It's not our enemies that are at issue. It's me. If you stretch one more time, pulling that T-shirt tight across those luscious breasts of yours or tightening your pants across that curvy little ass, I may have to handcuff myself so I'll keep my hands off you."

She blinked, then swallowed, understanding now why he was so tense, his eyes so dark. His hunger for her was palpable, his hands fisting in the comforter as his gaze slowly traveled over her face, her breasts, down, down, down. His Adam's apple bobbed in his throat. When a small bead of sweat rolled down the side of his face, she licked her suddenly dry lips.

Lance groaned and started gathering up the papers on

his bed. "You can stay here tonight. No need for both of us to leave. I'll grab a change of clothes and get a hotel room down the highway. In the morning I'll meet you downstairs and—"

She climbed up onto the bed and tugged the papers out of his hands. His gaze flew to hers.

"Keira, what are you—"

She tossed the stack of papers onto the floor and straddled his lap.

His eyes widened. "I wasn't kidding, Keira." His deep voice was raspy, sending shivers of desire straight to her belly. "You're playing with fire." He grabbed her by the waist as if to lift her off him.

She grabbed his wrists. "I'm a big girl, Lance. I know what I want. The question is, what do you want?"

His nostrils flared. "What I *don't* want is for you to have any regrets. We're both under stress, tired. We've been through a lot together in a really short time." His hands shook as he gently set her to his side and scooted back.

Her face flamed with embarrassment. "Okay, guess I totally misread the situation. No harm. No foul." She gathered herself to slide off the bed.

He stopped her and pulled her back across his lap, sitting sideways instead of straddling him. Even so, the evidence of his desire for her pressed thick and hard against her bottom. He stared down at her, and slowly, so very slowly, ran his thumb across her lower lip. She shuddered and closed her eyes. He rested his forehead against hers, his warm breath fanning across her face, making her shiver with longing.

"Keira, my desire for you isn't something I can hide."

"I'll say," she teased, slightly shifting on his lap.

He sucked in a sharp breath, then laughed. "You're killing me here."

"You're killing me. Mixed signals much?"

He groaned, then slid his hands around her and twisted to the side, setting her on the bed between his outstretched legs instead of on his lap. Then he gently pulled her back against his chest and loosely looped his arms around her waist.

"When this is over," he whispered next to her ear, "when I know you're safe, you're going back to your life in Maple Falls."

She stiffened and started to push away.

"Let me finish." His arms tightened around her. "Please."

She huffed out a breath, then leaned back against him. "What? Just say it."

"Don't be angry." He feathered his hands across her arms, massaging her taut muscles. "You're a breath of fresh air, Keira. You're smart, courageous, gorgeous, funny and honest. But this, us, it happened so fast, under extraordinary circumstances. Our emotions are running high. At any other time, I'd gladly accept the precious gift you just offered me. I'd be honored. But you're special. This…thing between us is special. It should be treasured, not rushed. We need to be sure it's as real as it feels right now. Making love is a line that, once crossed, changes everything. If we act without taking our time to get to know each other, we may later find that what feels real right now causes regrets later. Do you understand? Does that make sense?"

She pushed out of his arms and turned on her knees to face him. "You're saying you don't want me to wish we hadn't made love weeks down the road."

"Yes."

"There is no planet on which that could possibly happen."

He laughed. "Well, I appreciate that. And I wish I could be as sure as you that you'll still feel that way weeks from now. But I'd rather risk you being upset with me than to do anything that can't be undone later. I want us both thinking clearly and to be sure before we take a step like this."

She shook her head. "Wow. I didn't think guys like you existed in the real world."

He frowned. "What do you mean?"

"Just that… I didn't know there were…any gentlemen left out there. Men who value a woman for her mind, her personality, more than they want to jump her bones."

He choked on a laugh. "I'm not the saint you're painting me to be. The line I'm drawing in the sand is shaky at best. And the only reason I'm drawing it, to be clear, is because I care about you. I don't want you for just one night. I want it all."

She stared at him, afraid to ask what "want it all" meant. To her, it meant white picket fences and churches and babies. It meant forever. The thought of forever with him, with anyone, was the bucket of ice water she'd needed. It cleared her mind like nothing else would have. Because it scared her. He was right. They needed to take a step back, a huge step back. And explore a relationship at normal speed, not warp speed.

As impossible as it seemed, he might be right that in a week, two, more, when things were back to normal—whatever normal was—they might not feel the way they did right now. And, holy moly, neither of them had any protection. What had she been thinking? The repercussions of that could link them forever, even if they decided forever wasn't in their cards.

She slid off the bed and straightened her shirt. "Well. I'm glad one of us had the strength to stop things before they got out of hand."

He gave her a doubtful look. "Are we okay? Can we still work together as a team and this not cause problems between us?"

"Absolutely. Of course. We're both professionals." She cleared her throat. "I've decided to get a snack after all. I'm going to raid the kitchen. Want anything?"

He arched a brow. "I thought it was my job to ransack the kitchen."

"Yes, well. I'm not sure what I'll want until I take a look. If I see something really yummy down there, I'll bring you some. Deal?"

"Deal."

She slid her feet into her slippers and practically ran out the door.

LANCE STARED AT the closed door for a long moment. His heart was racing so fast he was surprised he wasn't having a heart attack. And his erection was so hard it was painful. Keira had no clue how difficult it had been for him to turn down her invitation. And while the reasons he'd given her for waiting to take that step were true, he hadn't told her everything.

Like that he didn't want to risk jumping into a relationship this quickly because he'd been burned so badly by Ileana.

He knew Keira wouldn't appreciate being compared to his ex. And he wouldn't blame her. But he'd fallen fast and hard before. And that had ended in disaster. He'd waited too many years for someone as special as Keira to come along to rush into things and possibly make another mistake. He was a different person now, a man instead of a boy. Mature instead of ruled by his hormones.

Or at least, he'd thought that, until he'd very nearly pounced on Keira when she'd straddled his lap.

Realizing he was so close to losing his control had scared him. It had him thinking about Ileana and the mistakes he'd made. Keira deserved better. She deserved a man who respected and loved her, not a man ruled by physical desire who didn't know his own mind. The two of them needed time. And they didn't have that luxury right now. They had a killer to catch and stop before he hurt or killed someone else, most especially Keira.

Ever so slowly, he slid off the bed and stood. He winced and adjusted himself, then headed into the bathroom for a long cold shower.

MORE THAN AN hour passed before Keira mustered the courage to return to the room that she and Lance were sharing. She hesitated in the hallway, her hand on the doorknob. She hadn't ended up getting anything to eat. Instead, she'd sat in the front room that the innkeeper called a library even though there weren't any books in it. She hadn't needed anything to read anyway. Her jumbled thoughts were enough to keep her occupied.

What had happened, and almost happened, between her and Lance had her confused and restless. But mostly, it had her frustrated that she'd allowed her wants and desires for him to get tangled up in what they were trying to do—find and stop a killer. All the times that the lieutenant back home had chided her for not staying focused or for being impulsive, she'd chalked up to him not taking her seriously because she was a woman. But just a few days into investigating this so-called mole, she'd let personal things cloud and distract her from the case.

Maybe the LT was right, and she wasn't ready to be a detective just yet. Surprisingly, that thought didn't make her angry. Instead, it had her thinking hard about those dues she'd wanted to avoid paying as she zipped up the ladder to get a coveted detective spot. Maybe she really did need more experience first. She needed to hone her skills and truly be ready before taking that next step.

As soon as she'd come to that conclusion, her mind cleared. A sense of relief swept through her, and much of the tension and pressure she'd been under for so long lifted. She wasn't sure what that meant for her future in law enforcement. Did she want to keep going along as she had been? Or was there something else out there she was more suited for?

Whatever the eventual answers to those questions might be, for now she was eager to get back on the current case and help Lance in any way that she could. Then, well, she'd see where things went, both professionally and personally. She just hoped she could handle the embarrassment of facing him again after practically jumping his bones earlier.

Straightening her shoulders, she drew a bracing breath and opened the door to their room. When she saw Lance standing by the bed looking at some pictures on top of the comforter, she hesitated again. He hadn't even looked up when she'd opened the door. He was dressed in some soft-looking plaid pajama pants and a dark-colored T-shirt. His short dark hair was damp and curling at the ends, indicating that he'd recently had a shower. But it was the angry look on his face that had her concerned.

She closed the door. The loud click had him looking

up. He gave her a brief nod, then looked down again as if still lost in thought.

When she reached the bed and saw what he was looking at, she winced. Although she'd been to a few autopsies, they'd always been a struggle for her to endure. These photos of Levi Alexander were no different. No wonder Lance was upset. Seeing his teammate and friend laid out on a metal table brought the loss home on a completely different level. It made it painfully real.

Thankfully, the black-and-white outline of a human body on the opposite page that indicated the wounds didn't show many. He'd been stabbed twice. In the abdomen. The other cuts and bruises were relatively minor, no other true stab wounds. And the cause of death was listed as exsanguination. He'd bled out.

She motioned toward the report. "Hopefully the speed and shock of the attack meant he didn't feel much pain."

He was frowning, staring down at the report. "It says he had stage four prostate cancer, which had spread to his liver and brain."

"That's awful," she said. "I'm so sorry about your friend. This all has to be such a shock. I can't imagine your pain, seeing Levi this way. He's a pale shadow of the vibrant man in that other picture you have of him. Maybe the cancer helps explain why he looks so different."

He gave her a strange look, then selected the photograph she was talking about and set it beside the autopsy photo. "You mean this one?"

"Well, yes. That's the picture we used all day when asking if anyone had met him."

He took another picture from the stack and set it beside the first. "What do you see when you look at this photo?"

"Happier, healthier times, I guess. In this one, Levi is

smiling. His face is fuller and his skin color looks much better."

His jaw worked. "That second photo isn't Levi. It's another teammate of ours, Sam McIntosh. And this—" he pointed to the autopsy photo "—isn't Levi. It's Sam." He looked up from the pictures, his eyes dark with anger. "Now I know why Levi was flirting with Ileana. It wasn't Levi at the café. It was Sam."

She drew a sharp breath and looked at the pictures again. Now, knowing they were two different men, she could see the small differences. But someone who didn't know either of them would likely do what she and others had done, including the waitress. They'd confused the two and thought they were one and the same.

"For Sam's body to have had Levi's ID on it, Levi had to have been involved and switched their identification," Lance continued. "I believe that Levi took advantage of how much he and Sam looked alike to fake his own death. Then, when Rick read about Levi's death, he must have come here and spoken to the police. When they showed him a picture from the autopsy report, Rick would have known it was Sam. Levi was either watching for any OPI teammates to show up, or he was hanging around town for some other reason. Either way, he knew that Rick knew the truth. So he kept tabs on him, made plans, then likely lured him to that motel in Maple Falls and tortured him, looking for information on the rest of the team. Then he killed him." His jaw worked again. "My old teammate and friend Levi Alexander is the mole."

Chapter Thirteen

Since Trent and Asher had told Lance that the team was working the case 24-7, and it was already late, Lance decided to call the main line to Unfinished Business rather than wake anyone. When the line finally clicked, a woman's voice came on.

"Unfinished Business, Ivy Shaw speaking."

"Hey, Ivy. How'd you get stuck with the night shift?"

"Lance! It's great to hear from you. How are things going? Is there an emergency? I can send someone to you and—"

"No, no. Sorry. Didn't mean to worry you. No emergency, thankfully. Trent told me you all were taking turns keeping the investigation going. Is anyone else there with you?"

"Callum will be back in a few minutes. He headed down the mountain to grab us some food."

"Let me guess. Pepperoni pizza and beer."

She laughed. "You know Callum well. For me, he's grabbing a salad. And breadsticks of course, with marinara sauce for dipping. A woman can't live on salad alone."

"You're currently trying to track down the OPI mole, right?" he asked.

"Yep. Making good progress too. We're down to two of the men on your list—Eli Pratt and Chris Landrew. Both are higher-ups in Homeland Security and held positions of power even back when you worked at OPI. It's looking promising that one of them at least had the potential to be involved, with the authority and opportunity to order or do the things you pointed out in your research."

"Homeland Security." Lance looked at Keira standing by his bed, watching him intently as he spoke to Ivy. "HS fits. They'd have the power, as you said. But more than that, back in the agency's early days, they'd have the reach and vaguely defined guidelines that were the rule more than the exception. I can see them having interests in many of the cases we worked that I later found out went south—for all the wrong reasons. Have you gotten any idea of the motive behind the breach? Money, revenge or power all work in this situation, I'd imagine."

"My vote is on money," she said. "It would be pathetically easy, as you said, during the inception of HS, to hide expenditures, mislabel and channel money to other items or people. But that's speculation at this point. As to deciding whether Pratt or Landrew is our mole, it's a toss-up right now. Maybe they worked together. We'll figure it out. Shouldn't take much longer. The information you amassed over the years was incredibly detailed. You'd have eventually figured it all out on your own. But I'm glad you trusted us to help you wrap it up more quickly. Is that why you called? For a status update?"

"Actually, I called to update you and the others. Keira and I have been digging into the deaths of my teammates, Levi Alexander and Rick Cameron. We've found out that there was mistaken identity that seems to have been intentional. Levi Alexander isn't the one in New York who was killed. It was another teammate, Sam McIntosh. He and Levi look a lot alike. We used to tease them that they could be brothers. I believe that Levi capitalized on that resemblance to kill Sam and take over his identity. Although, as to why he'd do that, I really don't know yet."

"Oh no. I'm so sorry, Lance. That's a heavy thing to deal with, grieving for one friend only to find out he's double-crossed your team and you have yet another teammate dead. Wow."

"It's been a surprise, for sure. Although it's nothing I ever considered before, having both a mole inside and outside of OPI helps fit a lot of the pieces together that I had trouble with while investigating everything that happened. Our missions came from multiple alphabet agencies and were vetted through our boss, Ian Murphy. What never made sense was that the murders of people we investigated were happening regardless of whether the mission was for the CIA, the FBI, Homeland Security or other agencies. I was trying to find someone with enough power that they could tap into the other agencies, maybe in conference calls with the higher-ups. If Levi was a mole inside OPI, he'd have the information on all the cases regardless of which agency it was for. He could then give that info to the agency mole, such as Homeland Security."

He shook his head, disgusted with himself. "I should have seen that years ago. But I trusted my team. I was blind to any of them being involved."

"Don't beat yourself up over it," Ivy said. "It's hard to be objective about friends, especially when they're your team that you rely on to watch your back and help you in dangerous situations. That objectivity problem is why we've been doing a deep dive into the backgrounds on each of your teammates. We'll switch gears now that we know Sam is gone and Levi is still around. With him stealing Sam's identity, he's definitely moving to the top of our priority list. I'll pass along anything we find out."

"Thanks, Ivy. Thank everyone for me. Keira was right to push me from the beginning to trust my UB family to help with this. Just be alert. Stay safe, all right?"

"You bet. Callum's pulling up in the parking lot out front. Want to talk to him about this?"

"I'll leave you to relay it," he said.

"No problem. Are you and Keira staying where you are or heading somewhere else to continue hiding out until we know it's safe for you to return to Gatlinburg?"

He held Keira's gaze as he answered Ivy. "I'll discuss it with Keira and we'll decide together. We'll keep you posted."

Keira smiled, no doubt appreciating that he was consulting with her now, rather than telling her what they were doing as he'd done at first. She sat on the foot of the bed, waiting for him to update her about the call.

"Lance," Ivy said, "you and Keira be really careful. I don't want to have to help train a newbie around here."

"Well, thanks for the concern."

Ivy laughed. "You know we love you. Later."

Lance ended the call and tossed the burner onto the bed. After he updated Keira on what Ivy had told him, she shook her head.

"It's beyond disappointing to think that someone high up in Homeland Security would use their power to have people killed to further their own greed or other objectives," she said. "My fear is that someone like that could no doubt spin a story to cover their tracks, even now. The guys who came after us were probably hired mercenaries without any traceable links to him. If he finds out that you've discovered Levi is his contact, he'll do everything he can to take us out. We're in a perilous situation, more now than before. I don't think we should stay here in Newtown any longer. We've been asking lots of questions. And Trent and Asher, even though the police and autopsy information they provided is helpful, it could also have put us on someone's radar."

He smiled. "On that we agree."

She arched a brow. "Which part?"

"All of it."

"Oh. Good. So, we're leaving?"

"As soon as possible." He pulled each of their suitcases out of the closet and set them on their respective beds.

Keira grabbed her clothes from the top dresser drawer. "Sounds like UB is well on its way with the investigation into Homeland Security. Are they trying to figure out where Levi might be too?"

He set his duffel bag of money, IDs and weaponry into his suitcase. Then he tucked his socks and underwear beside it. "Ivy said he's now at the top of their priority list."

When he turned around, she was watching him, concern evident in her expression. "You don't sound very confident. You don't think they'll find him?"

He shrugged. "I know they can and they will. Eventually. I just think I might have a better chance of finding him than them, now that I know specifically who to look for. UB can chase after HS. Our boss and our company have the type of connections to make the inquiries that I wasn't able to make when I worked this on my own. What I want to focus on is Levi. Something is off there. If he's the OPI mole, why would he trade identity with Sam and make it look as if he's the one who died? The only answer that makes sense to me is that he's on the run, hiding."

She checked the drawers, apparently making sure that she hadn't missed anything, her back to him. "You think he's fallen out with the HS mole?"

"That would explain why he's on the run." Lance took the few shirts and jeans he'd brought and quickly folded them. He and Keira had assumed they'd be here several days or he wouldn't have unpacked at all. "The mole probably knows everything about Levi, including where he lives. But Sam's identity ends here, in Newtown. As long as Levi doesn't go back to his own home or places he normally frequents, he has a chance at getting away."

"Right," she said. "As Sam, he's fresh, brand-new. It's a dead end for the mole to look for him as Sam anywhere other than in Newtown." She shut the dresser drawers and turned to face him. "But if HS doesn't know where to look for him, how will we know where to look for him? And something else is bugging me about all of this too. Why would your ex, Ileana, show up around here with Sam? Do you think she could be involved with what happened at OPI?"

"All good questions, Detective Sloane. Questions for which we need to get the answers."

She smiled at his use of the detective title. "Guess we'd better get busy, then, and find those answers."

When they were in his SUV, Keira fastened her seat belt and took a cautious look around, as if watching for a slew of mercenaries to come running at them. Her right hand was poised near where her gun was holstered beneath her jacket.

He hated that she had to be worried about her safety. She still felt guilty about coming to Gatlinburg and leading his enemy there. But none of this was her fault. It was his, for making the decision to run and hide all those years ago. If he could have a redo, he'd have dedicated himself to finding the mole, or moles, in the beginning. Then Sam and Rick wouldn't have been murdered. And Keira wouldn't be caught up in all of this, with her life in danger. Meanwhile, an incredibly selfish part of him was thankful that things had gone the way they had. Otherwise, he might never have met her.

"Since we don't know yet where to search for Levi," she said, "I'm thinking we should head to Tennessee, maybe the western region so we're close enough to UB for assistance if we need it but far enough away from Gatlinburg and Maple Falls that our enemies won't stumble across us."

He started the SUV. "Ever been to Kentucky?"

She blinked. "Kentucky? No. What's in Kentucky?"

"In the southwestern corner, there's a tiny one-light farm town called Wingo, population a little over five hundred."

"That's a really small town. I'm guessing they don't even have a motel. Why would we hide out there?" Her eyes widened. "Wait, I'll bet Levi grew up there. You think he might have returned to his roots? Wouldn't that be dangerous if the HS mole knows all about him?"

"It would be. Agreed. But Levi's roots are in the bright lights of LA. He wouldn't dream of living in a rural area like Wingo. He'd be worried he'd get horse or cow manure on his wing tips."

"Oh." She sounded disappointed.

"Sam, now, he's a different story," Lance continued. "He was born and raised in Wingo on a large farm. His parents grew corn, tobacco, soybeans. But it was their small stable of thoroughbreds that they raised for the sheer love of horses that he was so proud of. He took me there on vacation many times to go riding and show me the hundred-acre property that he loved."

"Wait, so you're thinking Levi—pretending he's Sam now—would go to that farm?"

"If he's desperate, it could be a first stop until he gathers his resources and figures out his next move."

"No, it would be foolish," she insisted. "Anyone could look up Sam's birth records and trace him to Wingo. The HS mole would think of that and check it out."

"I disagree. It goes against all logic and common sense to go to Wingo, which is why the HS mole wouldn't bother. He wouldn't think Levi was that foolish. Instead, he'll focus on trying to find Levi through other means. The more I think about it, the more I think Levi would hide out there."

"I'm not sure I agree," she said. "But if we do decide to go there, at least for a quick look, what about Sam's parents? Do they still live on the farm?"

"They passed away years ago. But Sam kept the property. I checked on it a while back as part of looking into finding the mole and doing what I could to ensure the team was still safe. Sam didn't live there, of course. He'd gone underground, new identity and all that like the rest of us. But he kept the land under a web of shell corporation names. He was too sentimental to give it up. It's rental property now, a farm that a management company leases out. With no one knowing Sam is actually dead, that likely hasn't changed. If Levi did decide to go there, he would have told the management company to clear out any renters so he could stay there. With enough cash, I imagine it would have been easy to make that happen." He glanced at her, his hands on the steering wheel. "It's all conjecture. But since we need to get out of Newtown—"

"Why not head to Wingo?" She smiled. "Let's do it. Let's go find Levi."

Chapter Fourteen

The drive from Newtown to Wingo took almost twelve hours. Keira was grateful that Lance had agreed with her that driving straight through without any sleep wasn't safe. They'd stopped at a hotel just before dawn, separate rooms this time. Keira fell asleep the moment her head hit her pillow. Lance had told her he'd pretty much done the same, except for a call first to Trent to update him on their plans.

With the sun beginning to sink on the horizon, they'd finally arrived at their destination—Wingo, Kentucky. When Lance told her that Wingo was small, she'd pictured a quaint Southern town with a square anchored by a historical-looking city hall sporting a clock tower on top. Surrounding the square would be little mom-and-pop restaurants, old-fashioned dime stores and antique shops. Instead, the "town" part of Wingo consisted of one street that was probably no more than a city block long.

At the top of the hill at the beginning of the street was a funeral home. The bottom of the hill boasted a handful of abandoned boarded-up stores, rusty railroad tracks and what appeared to be a clothing factory that might have been in use during the last world war. At the top of the other side of the hill was a church.

That was it.

Wingo, the town, had apparently died long ago. Wingo, the surrounding community, wasn't much to look at either. Or, at least, at first glance it wasn't. As Lance drove slowly down potholed gravel streets out to the paved rural two-lane highway, Keira was astonished at how friendly and outgoing the people were that they passed. And how *not* stressed everyone seemed to be.

No doubt, they all struggled like anyone else to go to work each day or work their farms, pay their bills, buy groceries. But they came home every night to a place where neighbors sat on front porches and called out to each other. Children tossed footballs beneath hundred-year-old oak trees in enormous unfenced backyards. Everyone they passed waved and smiled at them, as if they were lifelong friends. And the farms, they were nothing like she'd pictured in her mind either.

These weren't corporate-run monstrosities with miles of corn waving in the fading twilight. These were family farms, with thriving gardens up by the homes to provide fresh vegetables and spices. Chickens ran free across the yards, no doubt providing delicious eggs to their owners. And fences were used to keep the chickens and other animals safe from predators, not to keep the neighbors away.

She drew a deep breath of cool, fresh air through the open window, watching the quaint little homes as they drove past. And green plants that Lance had told her were soybeans, dotting the hills in neat rows.

"It's so beautiful here," she said. "Peaceful. No one honking horns or jostling past each other in a rush to go someplace else. I could get used to this."

He chuckled. "You say that now. But you may change your mind when you realize the only shopping around here is that mom-and-pop grocery store we stopped at a few miles down the road. Real shopping is a good forty-five minutes away. If you have a medical emergency, God help you. The closest hospital is even farther away. And I'm sure you noticed the lack of movie theaters and fancy corner coffee shops around here. They don't even have a bowling alley."

"Bowling? You don't have the potbelly to convince me you like to bowl."

"Ouch. I have a lot of friends who would resent that remark. No potbelly required. It's fun, especially if there's a pool hall attached."

"Ah, there we have it. The real reason you'd go to a bowling alley—so you can play some pool and down some beers."

He grinned, not denying her assumption.

"Enough with trying to ruin my fairy-tale impression of this charming town," she told him. "Okay, maybe you're right, and I couldn't live here full-time. But to unplug, disconnect and relax for a few weeks? Absolutely. It's really not much different than you living on your ranch, right? It's pretty far out of town. Isolated."

"The nearest Wally World is only fifteen minutes from my place."

"Ah. Walmart. The epitome of civilization. Twenty self-checkout lines and not a cashier in sight."

"Exactly."

She shook her head, smiling. "How much farther to the short-term rental you got us?"

"Another mile, maybe less. But Sam's place is down that next turn on the left. We could do a quick drive-by to see if anyone's home. It'll be dark soon. This is our only chance to get a look before morning light."

She straightened in her seat. "Let's do it."

"Windows up. The dark tint should help disguise who we are if Levi's there and sees us in the SUV."

They closed their windows. When Lance turned down the driveway to Sam's farm, instead of the gravel she'd expected it was paved and wider than the rural highway they'd just left. Maybe that was to make it easier on the horses when they had to be moved in or out of the property. She knew next to nothing about horses but didn't imagine a bumpy road would be good for them while keeping their balance in horse trailers.

With the sun setting, Lance turned off the headlights to avoid anyone seeing them from the house as it came into view. He stopped, and they both took in the lay of the land. Like everything else out here in the true country, Keira thought it was absolutely beautiful. The road continued for a good quarter mile across rich green fields to the one-story white farmhouse with a black shingle roof.

A porch with white railings and four brown rocking chairs ran the entire front of the home. White three-rail fences, like those at Lance's place, lined the long driveway and split the fields into smaller sections.

"Those are the stables over there to the back left side of the house," Lance said. "I remember some large wooden outbuildings directly behind the house for storing tractors and other equipment, including the horse trailer. I imagine they're all still there."

"Why would they need tractors? The fields are all grass, not soybeans, or whatever else they grow around here."

"A riding mower would take weeks to cut these fields. You can do it on a tractor in a few hours."

Her face warmed. "Mowing the grass. Right. City slicker here. Guilty."

He squeezed her hand. "You're coming around though. Before long, you'll want your own chickens and a little garden to raise tomatoes."

She wrinkled her nose. "No chickens. And I prefer spinach to tomatoes, thank you."

He shook his head. "We'll have to work on that. No self-respecting horse rancher prefers spinach over tomatoes."

"Maybe you can train me in the ways of ranchers."

His mouth curved in a slow, sexy grin. "I can teach you a lot of things."

"Promises, promises." She winked, her face warming at her audacity to do so.

He laughed, and she looked out the windshield toward the house, her face flushing hotter. She'd never been one to flirt or tease like she did with him. Something about Lance brought her out of her shell and made everything fun. Here they were, essentially on the run for their lives, and he could make her forget the danger and actually laugh. That was a rare gift. But also dangerous. They both needed to focus right now. Playing could happen later. If she was lucky.

Her fingers dug into her palms. She *really* hoped playing happened at some point between them. She craved Lance like a drunk craved his next drink. And she wanted to find out what it was like to move past that one amazing kiss they'd shared. She had a feeling that being with him would be spectacular.

"I don't see any lights on in the house," he said. "No sign of a car or truck either, although he might have parked around back."

They both watched the place for several more minutes, but even though it was getting almost too dark to see, no lights came on.

"We'll conduct some surveillance tomorrow," he said. "Let's get out of here before I can't see the road without headlights."

He backed the truck up until they reached a wide enough spot beside the driveway to allow him to turn around. Then he flipped the headlights on and sped to the main road.

A few minutes later, he pulled into another driveway, this one short and filled with gravel. It ended in front of a small white house with a front porch only large enough to accommodate two small cane-backed chairs, one on each side of the door. It wasn't all that different from the other little cottages they'd passed. But it was just similar enough to another cottage in her memories that it sent a chill up her spine.

A few minutes later, they were inside, their suitcases sitting in their respective bedrooms. They'd have to share the only bathroom, but it was a Jack and Jill. They each had their own sink and toilet. The only shared amenity was the shower.

Just like the other cottage.

She waited inside the eat-in kitchen as Lance carried in the few bags of groceries that they'd grabbed at the mom-and-pop grocery mart just outside of town. Normally, Keira would have helped. But the queasiness and panic that had been building ever since they'd pulled up outside finally won. She pressed a hand over her mouth and ran for the bathroom.

Her misery as she threw up her lunch was compounded by embarrassment when Lance was suddenly kneeling beside her, gently pulling back her hair. She would have pushed him away, but her stomach wouldn't stop heaving.

A cool damp cloth pressed against her forehead, her cheeks, her neck. It felt so good that her embarrassment was forgotten. He held the cloth against her forehead, whispering sympathetic words. When her stomach finally settled, he started to wipe her mouth. Her face flaming hot again, she grabbed the cloth from him and took care of it herself.

He stood and helped her up. Without looking at him, she flushed the toilet and moved to the sink to wash her hands. When he again made no move to leave, she finally drew a bracing breath and glanced at him in the mirror. "I need some privacy now. Please."

"Of course. Call out if you need me."

When he closed the door behind him, she almost called out for him to come back. The intimacy of him seeing her in such a vulnerable and awful way was embarrassing. But being shut in the bathroom alone in this house was so much worse.

Desperately longing for some toothpaste and a tooth-brush, she gargled warm water over and over until her mouth felt clean again. Then she was out the door, run-ning through the house.

"Keira. What's wrong?" Lance called out somewhere behind her.

"Can't. Breathe. Air. I need air." She didn't even slow down. She threw the front door open and ran onto the porch, her shoes catching on the threshold. Pitching for-ward, she threw her arms up to try to catch herself. Lance managed to grab her around the waist and jerk her back, saving her from tumbling face-first down the stairs.

He turned her and clasped her tightly against him. "My God. Keira. You almost…my God." His hands shook as he held her, rubbing her back and resting his cheek against the top of her head.

His kindness, his strength, his obvious concern, had

her fighting back tears. Again. But she absolutely refused to cry all over him as she had at the bed-and-breakfast. Mortified on so many levels, she pushed out of his arms.

"What is it?" he asked. "Are you sick? Do we need to—"

"Drive forty-five minutes to a doctor?" She forced a wobbly smile, still fighting the urge to curl into a ball and cry like the young girl she'd once been before she'd been forced to grow up far too fast so very long ago. "I'm not sick. I'm…" She squeezed her eyes shut, drew a deep breath, then another. Feeling more in control, she opened her eyes. "I'll explain later, but…can we…can we please go somewhere else? To stay? I can't… I can't go back in there. I'm so sorry. I know it must have cost a lot to get this place on short notice. And you might not get your deposit back and—"

"Shh. It's okay." His smile was so sweet, so compassionate, it had her heart squeezing in her chest. "I'm blessed that I don't have to worry about money. And I should have consulted you about the rental to make sure you were okay with it before I reserved it anyway."

"What? No. I knew you were calling to reserve something for us. If I wanted to provide input, I would have. I just…it never dawned on me that the place we got would remind me…would look like…" She shook her head and wrapped her arms around her middle. "Just please take us to a different house, one that's nothing like this one. Okay?"

He pressed the sweetest kiss against her lips. "If my marching orders are to get us a place nothing like this one, then that's what I'll do. No worries. Come on." He took her hand in his and led her to the truck, helping her inside and buckling her seat belt as if she were a precious gift, not the burden she knew she'd become.

"Give me a couple of minutes to call the rental agency again and grab our suitcases and groceries. I'll be right back."

She gave him a shaky smile and nodded her thanks. After he shut the passenger door, she immediately pressed the lock, not even caring that he must have heard it and thought she'd lost her mind. He jogged up the porch steps, and a moment later the porch lights came on. But they weren't bright enough to reach much beyond the porch itself.

As she waited, she huddled against the seat, her hand on her holster. She'd forgotten how dark it could be out in the middle of nowhere, without streetlights or the so-called light pollution of a city close by. And she'd forgotten just how oppressive that darkness could be.

When she realized she was sliding down in her seat, huddled like a child, she swore and forced herself to sit straight. She wasn't that miserable young girl anymore. And there was no reason to be afraid of an empty house. There were far scarier things to be afraid of right now, like Levi Alexander and whoever he might be working for to try to kill Lance and her.

Funny how so many years had gone by and it was still her past that had the power to frighten her far more than her present. Facing gunmen as an adult, using her police training and excellent marksmanship to protect herself and potentially Lance, was something she was prepared for. She could control her reactions, and how she approached the situation. It was the nightmares of her childhood that she still didn't know how to control.

A few minutes later, Lance jogged down the steps with

their two suitcases. He stowed them in the back of the SUV. One more trip into the house and he had the grocery bags. The porch light clicked off, and he hurriedly set the bags in the rear seats.

"Everything's set," he assured her, with an encouraging smile. "The next place is a bit farther, about five miles down the highway. We'll be there in a few minutes."

She watched in relief as the eerie cottage faded into the darkness. When the new rental house came into view, the tension in her shoulders began to ease. But the guilt inside her flared to life. This was definitely not a cottage. One of the more prosperous families in the area must own this one. Or a city slicker had it built as their summer vacation home. It was as modern as the other house was historical. Two stories of glass and steel were softened by gray ledge stone and cedar posts holding up the overhang above the double front door. Landscape lighting chased away the darkness.

Lance cut the engine and gave her an inquiring look. "Better?"

She unfastened her seat belt and impulsively kissed his cheek. "Much."

He grinned. "I can find a bigger house if it will get me a kiss on the lips."

Without missing a beat, she raised on her knees and pressed her lips to his. He groaned and picked her up, lifting her over the middle console and onto his lap as if she weighed nothing. Their first kiss had been full of heat and wonder. This one was scorching. She answered his every touch with her own, their bodies deliciously in sync with each other. He slid a hand around her back and one in her hair and deepened the kiss.

The honk of the horn as her back pressed it had both of them jerking apart. They burst out laughing.

"Talk about a mood killer," he teased. He popped open the door, lifting her in his arms and hopping down from the SUV. When she was standing in front of him, he leaned down and gave her another quick kiss. "The lock code for the front door is 4371. Let's check it out and make sure you're okay with everything before I bring our things inside."

"No. It's fine. Really. You did great. It's nothing like the other place. I'll grab the groceries if you don't mind getting the suitcases."

"All right, but if you change your mind about the house, I can—"

"It's perfect. Let's hurry. It's cold out here."

"Personally, I'm burning up." He winked.

Her face flamed as it did so often around him, and he laughed in response.

The house was everything the outside promised it to be. Clean, bright, open and modern. There was absolutely nothing to make her feel claustrophobic or remind her of her past. But since those dark images had already been resurrected, they were fighting to consume her. She doubted she'd get much sleep at all tonight.

While Lance put their suitcases in two of the bedrooms upstairs, she put away their groceries. There were snacks, peanut butter and jelly, crackers, bread, soup, beer, bottled water. And coffee of course, along with powdered creamer and sugar. Things that didn't need refrigeration. Neither of them planned on being in town long. A few days at most, less if they found Levi right away.

When she finished and turned around, Lance was a few yards away leaning against the massive dark quartz island.

"Are you hungry? I can make us some soup and sandwiches."

"I'm starving, actually. I'll heat the soup and—"

"I'll make the ribbon sandwiches."

"Ribbon sandwiches? Fancy name for a PB&J. Did you learn that in home economics class at school?"

"Actually, Mamaw, my grandmother on my father's side, showed me. You'd be amazed at my culinary skills. I can boil water too."

She laughed, and soon they'd both wolfed down their small hastily thrown together meal. Once the kitchen was clean again, they dried their hands on a kitchen towel.

"Seems rude to eat and run," she said. "But I'm practically asleep on my feet. Which bedroom is mine?"

"Top of the stairs, first room on the right."

"Thanks. For everything." She started past him, but he tugged her hand, pulling her back toward him. She looked up in question.

"Do you want to talk about it?" His voice was gentle, soothing, his expression one of concern.

She'd managed to avoid a discussion about why she'd panicked at the cottage. Dinner had consisted of small talk and plans for tomorrow's surveillance. But it was only fair to explain. She opened her mouth to do exactly that, but the shadows swirled in her mind, stealing the words.

"Just know that I'm here if you ever need to talk." He kissed the top of her head. "I'm not quite ready to call it a night. I'm going to log in to UB to check on their progress with the investigation, maybe catch a football game rerun. Sleep well." He headed into the main room with its U-shaped arrangement of black leather couches facing an enormous television on the far wall.

She flipped off the lights in the kitchen, leaving the

dimmed canned lights in the main room as the only lights on downstairs. "Lance?"

He'd just picked up the laptop that he must have set on the coffee table after taking their luggage upstairs. He arched a brow in question.

"Thank you. For everything."

He smiled. "Anytime, Keira. Anytime at all."

Chapter Fifteen

A slight movement had Lance opening his eyes and sitting up, surprised to find that he'd dozed off in the family room. He was even more surprised to see Keira sitting beside him, facing him with her legs crossed in her lap. Her hair was mussed, giving her a sexy just-got-out-of-bed appearance. But the pink pajama tank top and shorts with cartoon cats all over them had him grinning.

"Nice pj's."

She didn't even crack a smile. It was then that he realized how pale she looked.

He glanced up the stairs, his hand automatically going to the gun still holstered on his hip. "Did you hear something? See someone through the windows?"

"What? No. No, I haven't heard or seen anyone. No one real anyway. Or, at least, not anymore." She threaded her fingers through her hair, mussing it even more. "Sorry. I know I'm not making sense. I just, well, I couldn't sleep. Or when I did, the nightmares came again." She drew a shaky breath. "I can't remember the last time that happened. Years, I suppose."

"I'm a little lost here."

She sighed heavily, her hands nervously clenching and unclenching each other. "I owe you an explanation about earlier. The cottage."

He shook his head. "No, Keira. You don't. Everyone has demons they deal with, something from their past or some kind of phobia. That's for you to tell or not. Completely up to you."

"Okay, well. I need to tell you. I don't want you thinking I'm losing my mind. I want you to understand."

"All right. Take your time. Whatever you need."

She twisted her hands together, then turned, sitting close beside him, her right thigh snuggled up against his left one, warming him through his jeans. He swallowed, his entire body heating as she tentatively clasped his hand with hers and rested their joined hands on her thigh. She obviously had no idea how much he wanted her, how the simple feel of her pressed against him had blood flowing to all the wrong parts. Hating himself for even thinking about sex when she was obviously struggling to gather her thoughts and tell him something important, he used his free hand to pull a light blanket off the back of the couch.

Lifting their joined hands, he settled the blanket over both their laps and then set their hands back on top.

"Thank you," she murmured, no doubt thinking he was just worried about her being cold.

He tried to relax against the back of the couch, a bead of sweat running down his temple. But at least she couldn't see his painful erection straining against the front of his jeans with the blanket covering him.

When she still didn't say anything, he was about to remind her that she didn't have to and they could just sit quietly until she was ready to go to bed again. But her soft, hesitant voice broke the silence first.

"I was fifteen," she whispered.

And just like that, those three little words killed the desire flooding through his veins. Instead, he was now filled with dread, hoping, praying that she wasn't going to say what he feared she would say—that someone had hurt her when she was little more than a child.

Please, don't let it be that.

She rested her head against him. He automatically pulled his hand free from hers and settled his arm around her shoulders, drawing her close. She didn't pull back. Instead, she nestled into the crook of his arm. He wanted nothing more than to protect her, to keep her safe. But he knew that whatever she was about to tell him wasn't something he could save her from. It had already happened.

"I'd stayed a few minutes late with my algebra teacher, getting help with a homework problem. Missed the bus. Home was only a couple of miles away. At the time I was on the cross-country team, so I didn't bother calling my parents for a ride. I changed into my running shoes and took off jogging down the road. I can't tell you how many times my dad warned me not to run with earphones in both ears. He said it was dangerous, that I couldn't hear if a car was getting too close, that I should always keep one ear uncovered. Of course, I ignored his advice. Music was jamming. I never heard the van."

His stomach tightened. "Did it hit you?"

"I wish that's all that had happened. No. The driver parked on the side of the road, then came up from behind and grabbed me. I kicked and scratched for all of about fifteen seconds. He shoved a needle in my neck and everything went black. When I woke up, I was tied up in the back bedroom of a little cottage like the one we went to earlier tonight."

He swore softly and rubbed his hand up and down her arm.

"I won't... I won't go into the particulars. I did that in

court, and it was like being violated all over again. I never want to relive it like I did those three days on the witness stand."

"You don't need to," he whispered against the top of her head. "You don't have to."

She nodded against his chest. "I know. But I wanted you to understand. He held me captive for fifty-six days. Tied up most of the time. Kept in a darkened, tiny room. Only let out to shower when I stank too much for him to be able to stand me."

"Good grief," he said. "He was a monster."

"Yes. He was. And it was only through luck that I was eventually rescued. He was pulled over in town for a traffic violation when he was picking up supplies. An observant policeman remembered a witness's description of the van and a girl jogging on the side of the road the day I went missing. They'd driven by, not thinking anything of it until they saw the missing-person posters a few days later. If they hadn't reported it, and the policeman hadn't been suspicious, and my abductor hadn't been dumb enough to have kept my purse in his van, I wouldn't have made it."

She slid her arms around him, holding tight. "I wasn't the first girl he'd taken. But I was the last. And the only one who survived."

His hands shook as he lifted her onto his lap and held her like the precious gift that she was. Barely contained fury roared through his veins. The need to feel the monster's bones crunching beneath his fists was palpable. "What happened to him?"

"He was convicted and sentenced to life, without the possibility of parole. But he never served a day in an actual prison. He took the coward's way out, hung himself in the county jail."

"Good. I don't like the idea of you both sharing the same planet together."

She pulled back and smiled up at him. "Here I am thinking about the most horrific period of my life, and you have the power to make me want to laugh. You're an amazing man, Lance Cabrera."

He softly kissed her but couldn't dredge up a smile of his own. "You're an amazing woman. To have gone through what you did and have gone on to be a functioning, contributing member of society is an achievement of its own. To become a police officer, to face the evil others do day in and day out after experiencing the worst of the worst, is awe-inspiring." He pulled her close again. If she didn't need a hug right now, he sure as heck did. He wished he could take away all the hurt. But all he could do was be there for her. For now, hopefully it was enough.

"That's why you didn't want to go into the basement at the cabin," he said, his cheek pressed against the top of her head. "I imagine you're not a fan of dark, tight spaces."

"And being trapped. No windows or doors."

He winced and pulled back. "I was being stubborn, thinking I knew what was better for you than you knew yourself. I never should have locked you in that basement."

She smiled again, the color slowly coming back into her cheeks and the light returning to her brown eyes. "Apology accepted. You're a strong man used to being the protector. I get that. And I appreciate it. But as you said, I'm a cop. I've been trained and I can shoot pretty darn well, top of my class for marksmanship at the academy. We need to trust each other. As a team, we're much more capable than on our own."

He shook his head in wonder. "I've been on two significant teams over the years, and you're teaching me more about teamwork than I've learned in all that time."

"Slow learner, I guess."

He laughed. "Maybe so. I know I'm pushing my luck in asking any personal questions after what you just shared. But I'm curious about something else."

"I can't imagine anything more personal than what I've already shared. Go ahead."

"Your family. You're estranged from them, right? Is that because of what happened to you? Or something else?"

Her smile dimmed but didn't go away completely. "The ordeal as I've come to think of it happened in Memphis. Everyone in town knew about it. I couldn't escape the cruel comments of other kids at school or the looks and whispers whenever I went anywhere else. My parents tried to protect me by uprooting the family and moving us to Nashville. My younger brother and sister blamed me for them losing their Memphis friends. My parents were overprotective and practically smothered me. Dad turned to alcohol, trying to drown his guilt for not having been able to protect me when I was abducted. I was miserable. We fought constantly and I rebelled, got into trouble. When I turned eighteen, my mother gave me an ultimatum. Straighten up or move out. I was gone that same day, never went back."

"That has to be hard, not having the support of your family anymore."

"No harder than you being forced to give up yours."

"We're both orphans, in a way. Maybe one day we'll both be able to move forward, overcome our pasts and reunite with our loved ones."

"Maybe," she said, sounding doubtful. "Or maybe we move forward by creating a new family. Or, ah, families."

Her face flushed a delightful pink, letting him know he hadn't misunderstood what was probably a Freudian slip. The thought of the two of them starting a family, together, having a real future as a couple, should have scared him. His last serious relationship, Ileana, had been so awful it had soured him on the idea of ever getting married or having children. And yet, that kind of future with Keira didn't sound like a life sentence. Instead, it sounded more like winning a lottery.

She carefully stood, suddenly seeming shy as she adjusted her pajama shorts and then crossed her arms over her chest. "Seems like I'm always thanking you. But I really do appreciate everything you've done, how protective, strong and kind you've always been to me. And for listening. It helped. Talking to a therapist, a stranger, never seemed to work. But telling you just a little about what happened feels…like a weight dragging me down has been lightened considerably."

"I'll always be here for you, Keira. I mean that. Always."

Her eyes widened. Had he frightened her? Or was she surprised—in a good way? Before he could try to reassure her, she called out a hurried good-night and rushed up the stairs.

Chapter Sixteen

Keira was feeling raw and off-kilter the next morning. Her emotions were far too close to the surface, and it was difficult to concentrate. She was frightened of the situation that she and Lance were in, worried about some as yet unknown enemy wanting to kill them. Concern for Lance, in particular, weighed heavily on her. He'd become so important in such a short amount of time that she was more worried about his safety than her own. Part of that was because she felt that she was in over her head, both personally and professionally.

Her law enforcement experience was nothing compared to Lance's. She was good with a gun. And she'd always had a knack for setting witnesses at ease when talking to them as part of her beat-cop duties. But her detective skills were nowhere near what she'd once falsely believed them to be. The tips and suggestions that the UB investigators had given her seemed obvious—after they pointed them out. And Lance's suggestions did as well. But their ideas had never been her ideas. They'd never even occurred to her.

The longer she worked this case, the more she was beginning to accept that maybe being a detective, or even a cop, wasn't the right fit for her. And she was finally starting to understand why. After giving Lance a watered-down version of the trauma she'd endured as a young teenager, it had dawned on her, a real light-bulb moment, that maybe the whole idea of being a cop was just her response to that trauma. Being in control and making her own decisions were crucial to her feeling calm, to staving off the panic that was never far from the surface. Maybe working in law enforcement was just her way of maintaining that sense of control. It helped her feel stronger, less vulnerable. But did it make her happy? Fulfilled? Maybe she'd been wanting the detective title as just another way to try to search for whatever would fill the empty void inside her.

It was something to think about.

As to her personal dilemma that circled around Lance and her feelings for him, they obviously were attracted to each other. But in spite of the teasing and flirting they did so often, one or both of them always seemed to find an excuse or a reason to stop before they crossed a physical line they couldn't uncross. Was it because they really weren't meant for each other? Or was it simply because each of them was unsure of what their own future might look like once this current crisis with Levi and the other mole was over?

It was all so confusing. And it made it hard to focus and do a good job backing up Lance when her thoughts were such a jumble. But at least after pouring her heart out to him last night, she'd been able to get some much-needed sleep. For the first time since the attack at her Gatlinburg cabin, she felt rested and ready to face whatever obstacles were in their way. She just had to lock up the distracting thoughts about her career and Lance, and focus on their mutual goal of stopping the mole, or moles, and reclaiming their lives. The sooner they could do that, the sooner she could make some decisions about her future.

In spite of her worries that things might be awkward between them when she finally came downstairs freshly showered and ready for the day, things weren't awkward at all. After a quick, light breakfast and easy conversation, they headed out to Sam's farm to spy on it and see whether there were any signs that Levi was there.

They parked at the back of the property this time, using a road that Lance knew about from his many times visiting with Sam. From the way the tree branches and bushes encroached on the road, it was obvious that the most recent occupants of the farm didn't use the back entrance. So it was easy to drive up fairly close to the outbuildings in the woods behind the house and not worry about being seen. From there, it was a long boring day of watching and waiting for signs of life from the house, with just a couple of breaks to head out for something to eat and much-needed bathroom trips. Once back at the rental that evening, they'd used their respective laptops to look for clues about the fiasco that OPI had become.

The only thing of note that happened both days was that a man arrived at the stables in the mornings to feed the horses and turn them out into a pasture. Around the dinner hour, he showed up again and bedded the horses down in the stables for the night. But he never approached the house or any other outbuildings. And there were never any signs of life from the house itself.

The surveillance lasted two days. Both were essentially carbon copies of each other. No lights came on in the house. The blinds on the windows stayed closed. No one drove up the driveway toward it and no one came outside.

At the end of the second day, Keira and Lance sat down

at the kitchen table to eat dinner. Keira had slow-cooked a Crock-Pot of roast with potatoes and carrots, thanks to a trip to the little market for more supplies the day before. They'd both realized that living on peanut butter and jelly sandwiches wasn't going to cut it, even for a short stay.

Lance set his napkin on his plate and leaned back in his chair. "Either I was starving, or you're one fine cook, Ms. Sloane."

"Probably a little of both. I can steer my way around a kitchen when I want to. And we're both tired of junk food." She reached for his empty plate to rinse and wash, but he stopped her.

"I'll clean the kitchen," he said. "It's the least I can do after you cooked this delicious meal. But let's get our daily call to Trent out of the way first. I'm hopeful he's found something. We're coming up with zero on our end."

"Works for me." She moved their plates out of the way and sat beside him.

Lance got Trent on the phone and put it on speaker mode while they gave him their updates—which was basically that they'd made no progress.

Lance added, "I also tried tracing both Sam and Levi's phones that I had programmed into my computer. But regardless of which phone Levi was using when I sent the warning to my team to go underground, he's not using it now. It's either turned off or has been destroyed."

"We tried the same thing here," Trent said. "Even went through the phone carriers for their official records, courtesy of a subpoena secured by Chief Russo. Your team is well trained to ditch phones and switch to burners, is all I can say. We came up empty. This Levi character has gone completely off the radar. He hasn't returned anywhere that we've been able to trace him to in his past.

And from what you've said, he hasn't gone to Sam's one hold-out property from his early life either. As much as I hate to say it, we're at a dead end on finding him unless something happens to expose his location. Are you going to perform surveillance tomorrow or switch gears?"

Lance motioned toward Keira. "What do you think?"

She shrugged. "Without another lead to chase on Levi, I'm inclined to give it one more day."

"One more day it is then," he agreed. "After that, we'll need to find a new location to keep ourselves off the radar. Even though we're using alias internet accounts, cash and burner phones, we're still leaving an electronic trail. That makes me nervous. I'd rather head out sooner than later. But I agree with Keira that one more day feels right. I really thought Levi would show up here. And I don't have any more ideas on where to look for him at the moment. Any updates on the Homeland Security link?"

"Good and bad news on that front. The good news is that we finished our investigation into both of the HS guys we'd zeroed in on. The bad news is that neither of them are the mole. We're going to have to look at everything again, see if we missed something. One thing that has come out of this is that we did deep dives into the cases you'd researched where people were killed, the ones you and your team provided intel about. Although it's not obvious at first, when you peel back the layers, you'll find that many of the people who were killed had alleged links to organized crime. If that's the common thread, then a mole in the Justice Department makes far more sense than someone in Homeland Security. He could be in the FBI or even the US Marshals, turning over locations of witnesses to a mob boss to take them out. Making this entirely about money for the moles. They get rich, the mob protects its own people, who would have gone to prison if the witnesses had been around to testify."

"FBI," Lance said. "I looked at them but found nothing."

"Like I said, we had to go deep. We've used Chief Russo's influence, our TBI liaison and his connections to the Florida Department of Law Enforcement, as well as our boss's considerable influence on governors and other politicians. It's only through their hard work that we've gotten the subpoenas we needed, in record time I might add. And because of that we got access to information you and I would never have gotten otherwise. You wouldn't have found that link on your own. Trust me."

"I still hate that I didn't. I'll look at my FBI interactions in my OPI files again and see if I can pull any threads."

"Sounds good."

Lance motioned to Keira. "Anything you want to add? Suggestions on how to move forward?"

She cleared her throat, nervous about bringing this particular item up.

Lance smiled. "Whatever you've found, don't worry about sharing it. You might have figured out a clue that will put all the pieces together."

"Doubtful, but okay. I do have one thing I wanted to mention. And the only reason I'm bringing it up is because of Trent mentioning the Justice Department. That could mean any link to the FBI is important for the case, so—" she drew a deep breath "—something I was looking into last night, or rather someone, is, um, your ex-girlfriend, Ileana Sanchez. Or her married name now, Ileana Vale." At Lance's doubtful look, she rushed to explain. "I figured you might have had difficulty being objective about her, so I wanted to take a look just to make sure she's not the one who spied on the OPI missions. You haven't mentioned her when talking about who might have been double-crossing your team, so I—"

He held up his hand to stop her. "It's okay, Keira. You don't have to explain why you researched her. It makes sense to cover all our bases. The reason I haven't brought her up is because she didn't have any access to OPI case files. I didn't share my ID or password at any time. And I never discussed our cases with her."

"I would expect nothing less," she assured him. "But it's not you I was thinking could have had their access to OPI's computer system compromised, not on purpose anyway. She was with you for several years. She would have attended social functions with your team and their significant others, right? She knew them? Was friends with them?"

He was silent for a moment, then slowly nodded. "Yes. She was friends with them. But everyone knew the rules. No discussing our cases with anyone not on our team."

Trent chimed in on the phone. "Rules are made to be broken, Lance. You admitted you've kept up with your team as best you could in spite of agreeing that everyone would go their separate ways and not ever try to contact each other again. Maybe someone on your team stretched the rules too. Especially in the early days, before you realized someone was taking the information and using it to target people for execution."

Lance scrubbed his jaw. "Even if you're right, and she somehow managed to get someone on my team to talk about their cases, she wouldn't have had the power or connections to do anything with the information."

Keira cleared her throat again. "She got married shortly

after OPI broke up. The man she married is Hudson Vale. He currently runs the FBI field office in New York City."

Trent whistled. "If Vale is our guy, the mole, that just might be the connection we're looking for."

"I've never heard of Hudson Vale," Lance said, still sounding unconvinced. "Did you look into him too?"

She nodded. "He was an assistant in the same office as the FBI managers you looked into early on. While he wasn't at the top, he did have access, at least location-wise, to the offices of the big fish. If he's dirty, if he has relationships with those in organized crime, he might be someone we should look at more closely. Maybe Trent and the UB team can dig in and see if it pans out."

"Lance?" Trent asked. "If you feel strongly about this, I won't look into it."

He frowned. "Of course you should look into it. Keira did an excellent job discovering a potential link to some-one in the FBI who could be passing information along. But I'm still not convinced that Ileana would have the ac-cess to even get the information. There's only so much my team would have shared, even over a few pints of beer at a team gathering."

Keira twisted her hands together on top of the table.

Lance arched his brows. "There's more?"

"Just one more thing I wanted to mention that goes along with what you just said. Back at UB headquar-ters, when you were telling all of us about how you got started with OPI, you mentioned that you were following the criminology track in college. You also said that Ileana was majoring in information technology, computer pro-gramming specifically. I just wondered how good she was and whether she may have been swayed to put her skills into, well, hacking. If so, she could have hacked into your

OPI computer system. Did you two, um, live together at some point? Where she'd have access to your computer when you were gone or sleeping?"

His jaw worked, and the skin along it turned white as if he were clenching his teeth. Finally, he nodded. "We shared an apartment my senior year. And once I bought a house, she moved in and out depending on how our relationship was going at the time. I have no idea if she's skilled enough to have hacked into OPI's system. But she definitely would have had plenty of opportunities."

Trent filled in the awkward silence that had fallen over the meeting. "We'll jump on this and look into what Keira found. Should have at least an initial status update for tomorrow's call. Anything else?"

Lance looked at Keira. She shook her head. "No. That's it. Thanks, Trent." He ended the call and shoved the phone into his pocket. But instead of getting up, he remained seated, staring off into space.

Keira wasn't sure what to do. She could sense his anger, the tension in his body. It pained her that she'd done that, upset him. No doubt he was remembering his old girlfriend, both the good and bad times. Maybe the best thing to do was just let him be. Give him some space.

She stood and quietly took their plates to the sink. After quickly rinsing them, she loaded them in the dishwasher. She'd clean the rest later, once he left the kitchen. When she turned around, she jumped in surprise to see him standing directly in front of her. His face seemed drawn, his eyes a darker blue than usual. And his brows were drawn down in a frown.

She cleared her throat. "I'm sorry if I overstepped. I was trying to cover everything, make sure we hadn't missed a clue. But I probably should have asked you first—"

He ever so gently pulled her against his chest and rested his cheek on the top of her head. She was so surprised that she didn't even hug him back. She just stood frozen, not sure what to think.

"No, Keira," he murmured, stroking her back. "You didn't need to ask me first or apologize. You did exactly what I should have done and I'm glad that you did." He let her go and stepped back. "Any feelings I once had for Ileana died years ago. I'm not upset that you dredged her memory up. I'm upset that you felt you had to because I hadn't done my own due diligence. Not enough, anyway. I should have…"

He shook his head. "My point is that my ego wouldn't consider that I'd made any mistakes, or that my team had, to allow her—or anyone else—access to our files through any of us. I always assumed someone we did work for in the agencies, or their boss, would have used their meetings with my boss to obtain knowledge about the cases we were working. Making assumptions appears to be my downfall. None of the people I thought could be the mole have panned out. And now you've offered an entirely new avenue to explore as to how the information may have been leaked."

He finally smiled. "If you ever need a recommendation to help you with advancement to detective, I'll be happy to provide you one. You're proving to be a better detective than me."

She almost choked, then coughed. "Uh, no. I'm not. But I appreciate the compliment and offer."

He cocked his head. "There seems to be some hesitation there."

"I just, well, honestly I've been thinking that law enforcement may not be the right fit for me. The more I think about it, the more right it feels not to return to my old job. It was a way for me to heal, to feel I was in control after having that stolen from me so long ago. But I don't get the satisfaction at my job that I always expected."

"You have the skill set, Keira. Don't let anyone tell you otherwise. Maybe Maple Falls just isn't the right place to exercise it. Whatever you do, I hope you don't make a quick decision. Think long and hard before giving up a career that might end up providing far more satisfaction—in the right place, working for the right boss—than you might expect."

"I appreciate the advice."

"Or you're secretly thinking it's none of my business."

Her face warmed.

He laughed. "Now that all of that is out of the way, let's get to work."

"Right. Dishes." She started to turn and he tugged her hand, keeping her where she was.

"I already told you that I'm doing the dishes, cleaning up the kitchen. But that can wait. The work I was talking about is finding Levi. Even if Ileana is the true leak at OPI, I'm not convinced that Levi isn't involved too, or responsible for Sam's murder."

"Because he stole Sam's identity."

"Exactly. Watching the farm for two days hasn't gotten us any new leads. Rather than spend another day doing the same, I'm suggesting that we do some nighttime surveillance. Maybe he's somewhere else during the day and coming back at night. We haven't seen evidence of any vehicles coming in or out, other than the man taking care of the horses. But what if he's doing what we've been doing, coming in the back way? And only coming at night? It's something to check out. We can park somewhere outside of the property and walk in through the woods this time. And see if he shows up."

She glanced at the darkness beyond the kitchen window.

His warm hand urged her face back toward him. "If you don't feel comfortable outside at night, I can do this on my own. I totally get why you're afraid of the dark."

She shivered. "It's not the dark that worries me. It's the people who hide there. Plus it's extra cold tonight. Have you seen the weather reports? It might even snow in the early morning hours."

"Like I said. I'm fine doing it by myself—"

She lightly punched his arm.

"What was that for?" He mockingly rubbed his arm as if she'd hit him really hard.

She rolled her eyes. "You're not going by yourself. I'm your backup. We'll dress in layers and bring blankets. But if my feet start to lose feeling from the cold, we're leaving."

"Deal. Wheels up in ten minutes."

She laughed and they both headed for the stairs.

THE MOON WAS bright enough that they could see fairly well outside. That helped make up for the lack of lights on Sam's property. But two hours of being there, sitting on the cold ground in the woods behind the house, had Keira shivering. Lance swore and shifted around behind her, stretching his long legs out on either side of her thighs to form a warm cocoon around her. He pulled her back against his chest and wrapped both of them in the blankets they'd brought.

His warm breath fanned her cheek as he leaned down next to her ear. "Better?"

Oh boy, was it. The heat of his body warmed her all over, turning her hormones into a flood of lava in her veins. All she had to do was ease back, unzip her jeans, turn around and they could—

"Keira? If you're still too cold, we can leave."

"What? Oh, no. I'm…much better now. Thanks."

He bent down again, giving her a doubtful look. "If you shiver again we're leaving."

"I won't. I'm warm now." *Scorching.*

He watched her for a moment, as if waiting for another shiver. When she didn't, he straightened and wrapped his arms around her waist.

They sat that way so long she really was getting toasty. In spite of the pleasure in being held so intimately by him, she was about to ask him to move back a little before she started to sweat. But then a sound interrupted the night. It was a mechanical sound, a familiar sound but one that they hadn't heard since beginning their surveillance.

She turned and looked at him. "The condenser unit just kicked on."

He nodded, hurriedly pulling the blankets off both of them. "Someone turned on the heat. Let's see who's home."

A few minutes later, they were at the back door, one on each side, pistols drawn. Keira couldn't help comparing it to the same type of situation when she and her fellow deputies were outside Rick's motel room in Maple Falls. She desperately hoped they weren't about to discover the same kind of horrific scene.

Lance silently counted down, holding up his hand. *Three. Two. One.* He stepped back and delivered a vicious kick to the doorknob. The frame split and the door crashed open. They ran inside, pistols sweeping out in front of them. A dark-haired pale man was standing in front of a couch in the main room. Moonlight coming through the ruined back door illuminated the terrified look on his face as he stared at them in shock.

Lance aimed his gun at the man's head. "Make one move, Levi, and I'll kill you just like you killed Sam."

Chapter Seventeen

Levi didn't move, not even to raise his hands as Lance pointed the gun at him. Keira wasn't even sure if he was breathing.

"Light switch?" she asked.

Levi didn't say anything. He simply stared at Lance.

"Behind me," Lance said. "To the left. Unless the place has been renovated since I was here last."

The switch was right where he'd said. She flipped it on, and overhead pot lights lit up the main room and small eat-in kitchen area off to her left.

"Cover me," Lance said, holstering his gun.

"You got it." She aimed her pistol in Levi's direction, careful not to get Lance in her sights as he pulled the other man to his feet and searched him.

Lance took a pistol from Levi's front pocket and a knife from a sheath on his ankle. After putting them in his own jacket pockets, he ordered, "Sit down."

Levi slowly sat, his gaze flitting from Lance to Keira and back again. "If this is about Sam, I swear to the good Lord above, I didn't kill him."

"Right," Lance said, his voice angry, clipped. "You just happened to be in Newtown at the same time as him, saw him get killed, then switched IDs."

Levi's eyes widened. "That's exactly what happened! Except that I didn't just happen to be there. We were friends. I was visiting. We were walking down a side street, and a car with dark-tinted windows pulled up. The passenger window rolled down and—*bam bam*—Sam fell. I ran behind a building. As soon as the shooter drove off, I rushed to Sam. But there was nothing I could do. He was... he was gone." Levi's eyes glistened with unshed tears.

"I didn't have a clue who'd shot him or why," Levi continued, "so I switched IDs in case they were going to come after me too. Sam lives, or lived, in Newtown. So there was nowhere else to look for him. But I lived in Rochester. There were plenty of places connected to me if someone was trying to find me. I hadn't exactly been living off the grid. So I figured if I pretended to be Sam, they wouldn't know where to find me as long as I didn't go anywhere I'd normally go. I had to act as if I really was dead."

"They. Who is 'they'?"

"I don't know. I assume it's whoever was after us from our OPI days. I'd honestly thought we'd left all that behind. But since I didn't know anyone else who'd want to kill Sam, I assumed our past—OPI—had caught up to us. And without knowing how they found Sam, I didn't know if they'd know how to find me. That's why I went on the run, came here to hide out until the heat died down and I could figure out my next steps."

Lance watched him intently, as if weighing his words for signs of deceit. Keira didn't know Levi or what reactions were typical for him. But every word he'd said bore a ring of truth to her. She didn't think he had anything to do with his friend's murder, which meant he likely wasn't involved in the attempted murders of her and Lance in Gatlinburg.

"What about Rick?" Lance asked. "Did you kill him too?"

Levi shot up from the couch.

Lance pulled his gun out of his holster so fast it was a blur. "Sit. Down."

The tears that had been threatening rolled down Levi's cheeks as he sat. "Rick's dead? What happened?"

"You tell me."

"I don't know. I swear."

Levi was sweating and looking down as if ashamed. He was hiding something. But Keira still couldn't picture him having killed Rick. He seemed too devastated.

As if reading her mind, Lance said, "You're hiding something, Levi. If you want to survive the night, tell the truth. All of it."

Levi swore, anger darkening his eyes. "Enough, Lance. Okay? If you don't believe me and you want to kill me, just do it. I'm tired of being accused of killing my friends."

"What are you hiding?" Lance showed no reaction to Levi's anger and cut him no slack.

Levi swore again. "Rick was religious about staying underground, using aliases, burner phones. He was more careful over the years than Sam and I have been. But he showed up in Newtown after the news reported that I'd been killed in a mugging. And before you ask, yes, I hung around a few weeks after the shooting, and that's why I know Rick was in town asking questions. I was watching for that car again, the shooter. If he'd shown up I'd have taken him out. But he didn't. And Rick left soon after checking around town. I never saw him after that and I don't think he ever saw me. I don't know where he went. And I certainly didn't know he was dead. What happened?"

Lance stood in silence.

Keira took mercy on the frustrated-looking man on the couch. "He was shot. Much like Sam was."

He squeezed his eyes shut, in obvious pain. When he opened them again, his eyes were bloodshot. "Did he suffer?"

Lance slowly holstered his gun, signaling to Keira that he'd finally accepted Sam's story.

"I was there," she told Levi, "with Rick when he died. He went…peacefully." The lie was heavy on her conscience, but she didn't want to hurt this man any more than they already had.

Lance gave her a subtle nod, letting her know he appreciated her compassion.

He sat beside Levi and put his hand on his shoulder. "I'm sorry, man. When I found out that Sam was the one who'd been killed and his ID was switched with yours, I thought you must have been the mole inside OPI."

Levi frowned. "Mole *inside* OPI? I always thought one of the higher-ups in the alphabet agencies we worked with was the one who went after us. You think it was an inside job?"

"It's a long story. But Officer Sloane and I—"

"Keira," she corrected, smiling at Levi.

Levi nodded but didn't return her smile. He seemed shell-shocked by the knowledge that yet another friend of his had been murdered. She certainly couldn't blame him.

"Keira and I," Lance said, "along with some people I work with, have been looking into why our past has come back to haunt us all again."

"Us? Did someone go after you too?"

Lance nodded. "After Keira and me. She worked Rick's case. As I said, long story. But we believe someone in the

FBI, and someone either in OPI or close to someone in OPI, worked together to pass information to some organized crime bosses. My team is probably a few days from getting the evidence together to prove it."

"This is absurd. I mean, good that you think you're close to solving this puzzle after all these years. But crazy, and scary as hell, that someone in OPI is working against us. And coming after us again." He raked his hands through his shaggy hair, which badly needed a cut. "First Murphy, then Allen, Sam, Rick. Mick too, of course."

"Mick? He's dead?"

Levi nodded. "Just a few days ago, from what I heard. Cancer. Sam had cancer too. He wouldn't have lasted much longer, a couple of months at most. That's part of why he wanted to enjoy life, quit hiding. And it's why he reached out to Ileana. He was tired and wanted to spend the rest of his days with friends. He wanted to return to Wingo too, back to his horses." He shook his head. "Now he never will." He looked up at Lance. "You didn't know about Mick? Seems like you know everything else."

Lance shook his head, no doubt hearing the bitterness in Levi's voice but choosing to let it go. "I didn't know. There aren't that many of us left. Most of the team is gone."

Levi smiled for the first time. "Guess that makes it easier to figure out who in OPI was spying on us. But for the life of me, I can't imagine any of them—Brett, Melissa, Jack—leaking information to someone to murder people." Levi cast a bleary look at Lance. "I certainly didn't spy on us and pass along information."

Lance pulled the confiscated gun and knife out of his jacket pocket and held them out to Levi. "I know you didn't. And I'm sorry I put you through hell tonight. I needed to be sure."

Levi stared at him a long moment, then nodded and took his weapons. After he sheathed the knife and slid the pistol into his pants pocket, he asked, "You said you expected to have proof soon about who's behind this. Who's your money on at OPI? Brett, Melissa or Jack?"

"Actually, Keira has a theory about that, a solid one. We've been toying with the idea that it might be—"

Headlights flashed onto the front window blinds.

Lance leaned over the couch and peered between some slats in the blinds. "A car's coming up the driveway, fast."

"Only one?" Keira asked.

He nodded. "Just one." He watched while the lights flashed away from the blinds.

A few moments later, the sound of an engine indicated that the car must have pulled up right in front of the house. Then the engine cut off, leaving nothing but eerie silence.

Chapter Eighteen

A loud knock sounded on the front door of the farmhouse. Lance motioned for everyone to be quiet. He knew exactly who it was. What he didn't know yet was whether they were the mole or just another unpleasantry from his past coming back to haunt him.

He mouthed the words *Stay here* to Keira. Then, aiming his pistol toward the floor, he jogged to the ruined back door and slipped out into the night. He carefully circled the left side of the house to the front corner, using it to shield him from their visitor's view until he assessed the situation.

Headlights no longer shone from down the long driveway. The stillness of the night wasn't broken by the sound of idling engines from hidden vehicles. Moonlight didn't reveal any dark figures skulking through the pastures. The only sound at all was repeated knocking, pounding really, on the front door. And the sound of a voice Lance had hoped never to hear again in his lifetime.

"Levi, you're in there, right? Come on. It's me, Ileana. Open up. I need to talk to you."

Lance used her distraction to run behind the car, a dark-colored Mercedes. He peered through the back windows, then the front, although it was difficult to see much because they were tinted. No movement caught his attention. And no one shot at him. So the car was likely empty. Unless someone was hiding in the trunk, she'd come alone. Or there were more people hiding in the woods somewhere, unseen and unheard.

"Levi, please. Open the door!" Ileana pounded on it again.

Hoping he was right, that she truly had come alone, Lance crept up behind her. Going with his instincts, that she was the one who'd betrayed them all, he pressed the muzzle of his gun against the back of her head.

She froze, her hand in the air, ready to knock again.

"What do you want, Ileana?" he demanded.

She stiffened, then slowly turned around, eyes wide as she backed up a step. "Lance?" She looked past him, then left and right, as if expecting others to be with him. "What are you doing here?" She frowned. "And for goodness sakes, put the gun down. I'm not a burglar or robber or whatever you're thinking."

"You have no idea what I'm thinking. What do you want?"

She frowned at the gun he had aimed at her midsection now. "Can I at least lower my hands?"

"No."

She swore, calling him several unsavory names. It certainly wasn't the first time he'd heard them from her.

"I'm not going to ask you again," he warned.

"Oh for the love of… I'm here to see Levi. Is he here or not?"

The door behind her opened. Levi stood on the threshold. "I'm here," he said.

She whirled around. "Oh my goodness. You're okay? I

was so worried. I thought he'd killed you too." She smiled and held out her arms as if to hug him.

He held up a hand to stop her. "Wait."

Her arms slowly lowered. "What's going on? Why are you both treating me as if I'm a stranger?"

"Keira," Lance called out.

"Right behind you."

He glanced over his shoulder, surprised to see her emerge from a crouch behind the car, her pistol down toward the ground. "You followed me?"

"I'm your backup. One day you're going to learn to stop telling me to wait while you run into danger. It's never going to work."

"It appears that I'm a slow learner."

"You certainly are." She winked.

He chuckled. "I was going to ask if you would pat Ileana down."

"Pat me down?" Ileana practically shrieked the words. "What the heck does that mean? Who are you anyway? Lancelot's future ex-girlfriend?" She smirked.

"Officer Keira Sloane," she said, as she moved past him. "I need to check you for any weapons."

"What? No way. Don't you touch me, you little—"

Keira grabbed Ileana's arms and whipped her around, then thoroughly searched her. All the while, Ileana called her even more colorful names than she'd tossed at Lance. Keira straightened and held out her hand. "Give me your purse."

Ileana clutched it against her chest. "No. This is ridiculous. I'm leaving." She stalked toward her car. But as soon as she passed Keira, Keira snatched Ileana's purse.

"I assume your keys are in here," she said. "I'll return

this inside." She jogged up the steps and brushed past Levi, heading inside.

Ileana sputtered in outrage. "You have no right to treat me this way. You all have some explaining to do."

Lance holstered his pistol and motioned toward the house.

She huffed and marched back to Levi. "Are you really going to let them treat me this way?"

Levi looked at Lance, his expression unreadable. "Lance has his reasons. I'm sure he'll explain them to us." He put his hand on the back of her jacket and ushered her inside with him.

After one last look around, Lance headed in as well and bolted the door behind him.

"She has a gun in her purse." Keira tossed it onto the kitchen island.

"Yeah, well," Ileana said. "I'm a woman, traveling alone. Of course I have a gun, for protection. You're one to talk, whoever you are. Everyone here has a gun except Levi."

Levi didn't bother to correct her on her assumption that he was unarmed. "You have a black eye."

"Well thank you for stating the obvious," she said.

He stepped closer, clearly concerned. "How did you get that?"

She arched a perfectly plucked eyebrow. "My husband's fist. It's not the first time either."

Levi pulled Ileana to the couch and sat beside her. "You never told me or Sam that he ever hit you."

"It's not exactly something to brag about."

"Do you need some ice for that?" Lance asked, doing the right thing when he really wanted to throw some handcuffs on Ileana and interrogate her.

"Finally found your manners, Lancelot?"

He gritted his teeth. "Don't call me that."

"Whatever. No, I don't need any ice. Like I said, my... difficulties with my husband aren't new. And they're no one else's concern. That's not why I'm here."

"Why *are* you here?" Lance asked. "And how did you know that Levi would be here?"

The sound of running water had them looking toward the kitchen area. Keira had just wet a paper towel under the faucet and was wringing it out. She pumped a few drops of soap onto it, then took it to Ileana.

"What do you want?" Ileana frowned up at her.

"Proof." Keira rubbed the paper towel across Ileana's black eye.

Ileana cried out and shoved her hand away. "What the heck? Are you a sadist or something? Why did you do that?" She gently patted at her eye. "That really hurt, you little witch. And you've got soap all over it."

"I've been called worse." Keira held up the paper towel for Lance's inspection. "No makeup. She's not faking her injury."

Lance grinned. "Smart."

Keira smiled back and threw away the paper towel.

Levi faced Ileana on the couch, his expression one of concern as she continued to wipe at her eye. "Some... stuff is going on here. I'm sorry you got caught up in it. Now isn't a good time for a visit—"

"It's three in the morning," Lance announced. "She's not here on a social call. Why, exactly, are you here, Ileana? And how did you know that Levi was here?"

Levi frowned at the suspicion in Lance's tone but didn't interfere.

Ileana seemed disappointed that he'd let Lance speak that way to her. But she also seemed to realize that refusing to explain wasn't getting her anywhere. "I'd hoped that Levi was here. But I wasn't sure. I'd already looked everywhere else I could for him. And I called a million times without an answer. Either his phone is off or broken. This farm is Sam's family's place. I was hoping against hope to find Levi here."

She put her hand on his thigh. "I'm so relieved that you're okay. Hudson snooped in my phone and discovered I was having an affair with Sam. He shot Sam. And he bragged about it to me." She dabbed at both eyes this time, which were shiny and bright as if she were holding back tears. "When he saw in the news that you were killed in a mugging, he was furious. He said he must have gotten the wrong guy. He's been on the warpath ever since, trying to find you. He thinks you're Sam, with you two looking so much alike and all. If he finds you, he's going to kill you too."

"You came here to warn me?"

"Of course. What other reason would there be? Hudson is finally out of town on a business trip. This is the first time I've been able to get away in months." She motioned toward her black eye. "Of course he gave me this as a parting gift before he left, a warning not to go anywhere."

Levi patted her shoulder. "You should have told me about him." He winced. "Or told Sam. We'd have helped you. He might be a big shot at the FBI, but he's still going to get what's coming to him. We'll get justice for Sam, and for you. I know you really cared about Sam."

She sniffed. "Of course I did. Not telling both of you about what Hudson was doing was me trying to protect you. I wanted to take care of it on my own. But he found out anyway. And I couldn't… I couldn't protect Sam." She sniffed again.

"Is that true, Levi?" Lance asked. "Ileana and Sam were having an affair?"

Ileana rolled her eyes. "Of course it's true. Why would I lie?"

"Levi?" Lance repeated.

Ileana stewed in anger but didn't say anything.

Levi nodded. "Like I said earlier, neither of us was staying low under the radar. He saw something in the society pages in the *New York Times* about her one day. He'd always…always liked her. But of course, when you two were together, he never would have dared to act on his feelings."

"I know. Sam was a good guy."

Levi smiled sadly. "He was. Anyway, he was lonely, you know? He just wanted to see an old friend, a familiar face, again. She agreed to come visit in Newtown and, well, things progressed from there."

"Ileana," Lance asked, "how did you know it was Sam who was killed and not Levi? As you said, the news reported Levi as the victim of the mugging."

She shook her head in exasperation. "My husband was bragging that he'd killed my lover. Then he saw in the news that Levi was killed instead and was furious. I needed to know the truth, whether it was Sam or Levi who'd been killed. And I wanted to warn whichever one was still alive to hide from Hudson. What do you think I'd have done? Nothing? Just sit on my hands while my husband killed another one of my friends? What kind of person do you think I am, Lance?"

When Lance didn't answer, her face reddened. "Good grief. We had our bad times, plenty of them. But we had good times too. I don't understand why you're interrogating me like this. I had to go to the police in Newtown and look at that awful autopsy photo to confirm it was Levi. And then, of course I knew it wasn't."

"Did you tell the police that?" Levi asked.

"No, no, dear. I don't understand why you let people think that you were dead instead of Sam, but I assumed you had a good reason. Part of me wondered whether you knew Hudson had killed Sam and you switched places to try to keep Hudson from going after you too. After all, the three of us visited quite often in Newtown when Sam and I were an item. Hudson probably realized that when he snooped through my phone."

She sniffed again, although Lance didn't notice any actual tears.

"Once we get you somewhere safe, we need to switch that headstone in the cemetery," she said. "It's not right that your name is on Sam's grave. He deserves better than that."

Levi patted her shoulder. "He does. I agree."

Ileana motioned toward her black eye. "This thing hurts like the devil. Get me some ice. But first I have to pee, and clean the rest of the soap off my face. You're not going to try to stop me from using the bathroom are you?"

Levi held his hands up apologetically. "Course not. It's the last door on the—"

"I know where it is. Been here before." She glared at Lance. "Years ago, with my ex." She marched down the hallway and into the bathroom, slamming the door behind her.

Keira let out a long breath. "She's something."

Levi's chin raised. "She's a good person. She's obviously been through trauma with her husband and losing Sam. And it didn't exactly help that we held her at gunpoint when she got here."

Lance and Keira exchanged a long glance. He sighed and scrubbed his jaw. "Right before she arrived, Keira and I were going to explain that we believe Ileana may have used her computer programming expertise to hack into our OPI databases. With her marrying the head of an FBI field office later on, it lends more credence to that theory."

Levi shook his head. "No way. Whoever got that information is responsible, either directly or indirectly, for people being killed. Ileana would never want any of us hurt. That's why she's here. To protect me."

"Would you bet your life on that?" Keira asked.

Levi frowned at her. "As a matter of fact, I would."

"You saw her Mercedes out front," Lance said. "It's black with dark-tinted windows. Could that have been the car used by the shooter who killed Sam?"

His face reddened. "Of course it could have. Because her husband, Hudson, was driving it."

Lance and Keira exchanged another glance.

"What?" Levi demanded. "What aren't you telling me?"

Keira gave him a sympathetic look. "Lance and I were performing surveillance earlier, to see if you were here. Since Hudson Vale's name recently came up in our investigation, Lance tapped some resources and contacts that his company has with the FBI. Hudson was out of the country when Sam was shot."

"Levi," Lance said, "when Sam was shot, is there any possibility that a woman could have been driving the car?"

Levi's face turned pale. "I don't…maybe." He glanced down the hall.

"Ileana's been in that bathroom a long time," Lance said. "Keira, did you see a cell phone in her purse?"

"Ah, shoot. In her pocket. I noticed it when I searched her for weapons and didn't think anything about it."

They both drew their guns and took off down the hallway.

Lance busted in the door without even knocking. He swore when he saw the empty room, and the open window above the toilet.

Keira sucked in a sharp breath. "The mirror."

Written in toothpaste were three words.

You're all dead.

They whirled around and ran out of the bathroom.

Levi's eyes widened in shock when he saw them. "She's gone?"

"Out the window," Lance said. "We need to—"

"I'll stop her." Levi ran for the front door.

"Wait," Lance yelled, rushing toward him.

Levi threw the door open. The crack of rifle fire filled the house. Levi's body jerked as the bullets struck his body. He was dead before he even hit the floor.

"No!" Lance yelled. "Damn it. Not you too." He started toward his friend.

Keira jumped in front of him and shoved at his chest. "He's gone. There's nothing you can do for him. We need to get out of here." She tugged his arm, trying to pull him toward the back door.

He stood frozen, unmoving. Blood pooled beneath Levi's body. The door gaped open, revealing the moonlit front yard. And the sound of an engine starting up.

Ileana.

He started toward the door again.

Keira slammed her body against him, knocking him to the side a few feet, but he managed to keep his balance. "Stop it. She's getting away."

She slammed the flat of her palms against his chest,

blocking his way. "Wait. Listen to me. What if Ileana wasn't the one who shot Levi? You saw what she wrote on that mirror. Do you really think she would try to take on all three of us without help? She's not alone in this. Her hired hands must have just arrived and hid out front. Heck, she probably gave herself that black eye to get Levi's sympathy. Rather than her being a victim of domestic violence, I'd bet money her FBI husband is in on this with her. His men are likely out front right now. We have to—"

Another round of gunfire shattered the night. Bullets strafed through the open front door. Lance and Keira dove behind the kitchen island, low to the ground. As soon as there was a pause, they both jumped up and ran out the back door.

Chapter Nineteen

The rumble of more engines had Keira and Lance turning when they reached the woods, looking back toward the house. Three SUVs with gunmen hanging out the windows were barreling down the long road into the farm.

"Good grief," Keira said. "How many of them are there? We need help. A lot of help."

Lance shoved his phone in his pocket. "I just tried to call Trent. They're jamming the signal. We need to get out of their jammer's range."

They took off running again, crashing through the woods, leaping over the pallet of blankets they'd left from their earlier surveillance. They'd almost reached Lance's SUV when a flash of moonlight on metal had both of them stopping and ducking behind a tree. More vehicles were roaring up the back road.

"It was an ambush all along." Lance swore. "I'll bet all Ileana wanted to do was confirm how many people were in the house before she signaled her husband to bring in his mercenaries. Come on, this way." They took off running through the woods, leaving the back road and the house behind.

"What exactly attracted you to that woman in the first place?" Keira asked as she struggled to keep up with his long strides while scanning the trees for signs of gunmen.

He grinned. "I was young and stupid, and she had a figure."

"Men."

The sound of shouting off to their left had them jumping behind some thick pine trees.

Keira held her pistol in both hands, her lungs screaming for air as she tried to drag in quiet, short breaths to avoid anyone hearing her. Behind another tree, Lance mirrored her position, his chest heaving as he too tried not to make any noise. Very slowly, he leaned around his tree, then jerked back. He held up two fingers and motioned to his right. Then he held up two more and motioned to the left. She nodded to let him know she understood.

Could she and Lance take four guys out without being shot themselves? Possibly. Probably. She was good with a gun. And Lance, well, he was good at everything, as proven by his performance at the cabin. But eliminating four enemies when there were dozens out searching for them would only give away their location.

The sound of voices gradually faded amid shouts of a man somewhere behind them ordering someone to get some flashlights.

Lance leaned around the tree again, then straightened. He gave her a thumbs-up, then a rolling motion with his hand for her to follow him. The two of them took off in a jog toward the right end of the property in relation to the back of the house.

She was soon considering begging for mercy, desperately needing to stop and catch her breath. He was obviously in great shape, and their fast jog through the woods didn't seem to bother him at all. But she had a stitch in her side, her ribs were still bruised and she was gasping for air. There would definitely be more Pilates in her future, if she survived tonight.

Thankfully, Lance raised a hand and signaled her to stop so she didn't have to embarrass herself by asking for a reprieve. But when she saw why he'd stopped, she vigorously began shaking her head.

No, she mouthed, afraid to talk out loud in case any gunmen were close by.

He pointed at the building that housed the horses and nodded yes.

No, she mouthed again, shaking her head so hard her hair flew around her face.

Lance pointed in the direction of the house, mimicking a gun with his thumb and forefinger and firing over and over, reminding her they were severely outnumbered and had no choice.

And, dang it, he was right. They didn't. No matter how good a shot either of them were, they couldn't win against such overwhelming odds if they were discovered.

She glared her displeasure at him.

Sorry, he silently mouthed, then motioned for her to follow him again.

I can do this. I can do this. She silently repeated the phrase over and over in her mind as she followed him into the stables.

Taking everything one step at a time helped. She was the lookout at the door while he did whatever he needed to do inside. It gave her a task to focus on instead of wondering how in the world she was going to manage riding a horse when the closest she'd ever been to one before was at Lance's stables in Gatlinburg. Feeding a horse a carrot without getting your fingers bitten off was one thing.

Clinging to its back without falling was something entirely different.

Sending up a quick prayer, she pulled her burner phone out. *Please let there be a signal.* She pressed the numbers 911 and listened. Nothing but static. Dang it.

The sound of hooves shuffling against the hay-covered floors had her turning around. She immediately backed up, bumping into the doorframe as four impossibly tall horses surrounded her.

Lance appeared between them and grabbed her hand. "Come on," he whispered.

"Wait. Which one is mine? They don't even have anything to hold on to."

He grinned and whispered, "Saddles and reins?"

"Whatever," she whispered back. "I'll take my chances with the gunmen." She backed away from the horses milling around and started for the door.

Lance tugged on her hand. "Come on. We're not riding these horses. Those are the decoys."

A moment later she was standing in front of a huge black horse with a saddle and reins, as he'd stated. But there was no way she was getting on it. "It's huge. Way bigger than the others."

"That's why I picked him. He can handle both of us."

"Wait. Both of us?"

"You didn't expect me to ask you to gallop all by yourself when you've never sat on a horse before, did you?"

"Well, yes. I guess I did. Wait. Gallop? That's the really fast gear, right?"

He chuckled and put his foot in the metal thing hanging from the saddle. Then he vaulted up onto the horse. She stared at him, at his hand as he reached down for her.

"Sorry, I can't. I just can't." She hurried toward the other horses that were docilely standing just inside the door.

The sound of hooves clicking and stomping against the floor had her whirling around. Lance leaned down with both arms and snatched her around the waist. He swung her up behind him without even slowing down. Keira let out a squeak of fear as she landed on the horse's bottom behind the saddle and it gave a light kick.

"Hang on," Lance called out.

She wrapped her arms around his waist, locking her hands together against him.

"Hang on," he repeated.

She let out another squeak as the horse leaped forward. The other horses, the ones he'd called decoys, bolted out through the doors and raced toward the house. Lance jerked the reins of the horse they were on, and it dug in its heels, rounding the building and then taking off in a run deeper into the woods.

Keira knew she should have had her gun out and watched for anyone after them. But even if she somehow managed to hang on with one hand to free her gun, she'd never be able to aim it while bouncing on the back of this beast. She'd likely end up shooting herself, the horse or, worse, Lance. She suddenly realized that every spaghetti Western she'd ever seen was a passel of lies. No hero could manage this jolting, bumpy roller-coaster ride and manage to aim a gun at any bad guys. It just wasn't possible.

Bam, bam, bam.

Her eyes flew open, her ears ringing. Lance was holstering his pistol, having just shot it. She looked off to their left and saw two bodies lying on the ground, their guns dropped beside them.

Holy moly.

She blinked in shock and immediately revised her negative view of those spaghetti Westerns. Or, rather, she revised her view of Lance. He'd already been amazing. Now he was a hero in a whole other way. Her earlier fears dimmed and she straightened a bit, still hanging on for dear life. But no longer convinced they were definitely going to die.

Maybe they had a chance after all.

Bam. A gunshot sounded close by.

Lance suddenly arched against her. The horse whinnied as Lance jerked the reins. Then they were falling onto the ground. Her breath left her in a rush as she rolled underneath a scratchy bush, headlong into a mound of pine needles. Gasping like a fish out of water, she desperately tried to make her lungs work again. Her ears were as useless as her lungs. All she could hear was a low buzzing sound.

The horse bolted past her, its hooves flashing in the moonlight through the branches of the shrubs surrounding her as it galloped away from the house, minus her and Lance.

Where was he? He had to be near her, somewhere.

Her lungs finally expanded in a rush of cold air. She coughed and gasped, everything hurting as she got up on her hands and knees. What had happened? Gunfire. She'd heard a shot. Only one this time. And it wasn't Lance who was shooting. Oh God, please, no. Lance couldn't have been shot, could he?

The answer to that was brutally clear when some men shouted about ten yards away, motioning toward something on the ground. A man, a tall broad-shouldered man with a dark jacket and short dark hair. Lance.

A sob rose in her throat. She pressed a hand to her mouth to keep from crying out. Four men. There were four of them, poking at Lance as if he were roadkill. He suddenly moaned and swiped at one of the men's hands. Keira had never seen something so wonderful in her life. He was alive. Lance had either been shot or knocked out from the fall off the startled horse. But he was alive. Which meant there was still hope. It also meant that it was up to her to save him. She didn't know if she could shoot four men quickly enough to avoid being shot herself. But she was sure going to try.

She clawed for her pistol as two of the men grabbed Lance's arms and legs, hoisting him up between them. Her mind reeled in horror when she realized her gun was gone. It must have fallen when she was thrown from the horse.

Three more men, each holding rifles, joined the original four. They seemed to be arguing about something. Then they split up, some heading toward the house, others going in the direction that she and Lance had been riding. And another…coming straight toward her.

She bit her lip against the urge to cry out in pain as she scrambled around in the leaves, searching for her pistol. Everything hurt. She didn't think any bones were broken, just badly bruised, like her ribs that were really hurting again. But that was the least of her worries. If the man didn't stop or turn away, she was about to be discovered. And then Lance would have no one to save him.

The gun was nowhere to be found. And the man was getting far too close, scanning the woods near her. He didn't seem to know she was there. But he'd see her soon if she didn't do something. She continued to flail in the leaves, trying to find her pistol. Something sharp seemed to slice into her hand. She sucked in a breath, then pulled it up out of the leaves. It was just a stick, but it was thick and sharp on one end where it must have twisted and broken from the shrubs as she'd fallen. It was also slick with blood from where it had cut her hand. Stealing herself against the pain, she grabbed it and swung it up and out just as the man peered over the bushes.

It jammed deep into his throat. His eyes widened in shock, his hands clawing at his bleeding neck. Then he slowly crumpled to the ground.

Keira stared at his lifeless body, shocked that she was the one who'd done that. She'd never once shot anyone in the line of duty. And here she'd just stabbed one to death. With a branch. Hysterical laughter started to bubble up in her throat. She swore and forced herself to draw deep even breaths.

Think, Keira. Think.

How could she save Lance against dozens of armed gunmen with only a tree branch as a weapon? The answer was painfully clear. She couldn't. She had to get help. But how? There were men all through these woods. How could she escape all of them and make it back in time to help Lance before it was too late?

If it wasn't too late already.

She reached in her pocket for her cell phone, relieved when her hand tightened around it. Maybe she was far enough away that the cell signal was no longer blocked and she could call Trent or 911 or both. She pressed Trent's number and Send, then listened. The same buzzing sound she'd heard before sounded again. The signal was blocked. She'd heard somewhere that text messages went through better than calls when signal strength wasn't strong. She tapped in a quick message to Trent and pressed Send. Then she sent the same message to Asher. But both texts popped up on the screen with red exclamation points beside them.

Text failed to send.

She groaned and shoved the phone back in her pocket. Despair like she'd never felt before flooded through her. If she could trade her life for Lance's, she would willingly do so. But she was under no pretenses that the men after them would take that trade. They'd kill both her and Lance.

Lord, please. Help me figure out what to do. Give me a sign.

A whinny sounded behind her. She slowly turned around. The horse that she and Lance had been riding stood only a few yards away, calmly munching on some brown grass beneath a tree.

Keira swore and looked up at the sky. "You couldn't have given me a different sign? Like maybe a truck?"

As if in response, lightning cracked across the night sky. And it started to rain.

"Okay, okay. I won't look a gift horse in the mouth. Ha ha." She pushed herself to her feet and slowly advanced on the scary beast staring at her as if she were a bug it wanted to squash.

Chapter Twenty

Lance glared at the no fewer than ten men crammed into the small farmhouse's main room, milling around as the worst aggressor stood in front of him. No doubt him being tied to a dining room chair made Ileana think she was safe. She certainly thought so, the way she kept smirking at him and pacing back and forth. But she wasn't that confident, or she wouldn't be staying out of reach of his feet.

One step in the wrong direction and he'd sweep her legs out from under her. He'd follow that up by slamming on top of her, chair and all. He had every movement planned. But it was his last resort. Because the one thing he knew for a certainty was that if he attacked Ileana, every man in the room would riddle him with bullets.

Since there didn't appear to be a way out of here with his life anyway, the only thing really holding him back was Keira. When the bullet had grazed his head, knocking him silly, everything had gone fuzzy. He'd managed to climb out of the fog when he was being hauled out of the woods. But he had no idea what had happened to Keira. For her sake, he was trying to hold his temper. Stall. Do whatever he had to do to stay alive. Because if there was even one chance in a thousand that he could do something to help her, to save her, he would.

No matter how much torture he had to endure.

Ileana glanced at her phone again, her still-beautiful face drawn with impatience.

"What's wrong, Ileana?" he goaded. "Not allowed to make any decisions without hubby's permission?"

She scoffed. "Hubby? Are you kidding me? That weak, useless excuse for a man?"

"Ah. So you feel the same affection for him that you once felt for me."

"Shut up."

"If he's so weak, why are you taking orders from him? Why did you feed him information about OPI? Why do you let him beat you?"

She let out an angry screech and motioned to the man closest to Lance. He slammed his fist against Lance's jaw, whipping his head to the side.

Lance held back a groan. And smiled. The man raised his fist again.

"Stop," Ileana ordered. "I need him conscious and able to talk. Break his jaw, and he won't be able to answer my questions."

"I thought I already answered your questions," Lance said. "There are more?"

She stopped in front of him, her hands fisted at her sides. "You haven't answered anything! Where's the rest of your team? Where's Brett? Melissa? Where's Jack? Tell me and I'll let you go."

"Where's Keira? Tell me and I'll let you live."

Her phone buzzed in her pocket. She glared at him before checking the screen. Then she smiled. It was that smile that had him going cold inside.

"Bring another chair over here," she called out. "We're about to have company."

It took every ounce of control that Lance had not to shout in rage when two men stepped through the back door opening, dragging Keira between them. A chair was brought over close to Lance. And Keira was quickly tied into it, just like he was. Her head hung limply. Lance watched in terror for her chest to rise. Finally, it did. Thank God. She was alive.

Ileana was suddenly there with a glass of water. She tossed it in Keira's face.

Keira jerked in her chair, blinking at the water dribbling down her cheeks. She blinked again, then looked around as if only just then realizing where she was. She groaned, and Lance could have sworn he heard her curse beneath her breath.

"Hey, beautiful," he whispered.

Her eyes widened. Tears sprang into them and she smiled, drawing his attention to her cracked and bleeding lip. "My hero," she whispered back. "Glad to see you still breathing."

"I'm hardly a hero. But ditto on the breathing thing."

"Well, isn't this sickeningly sweet," Ileana said. "Two little lovebirds right before they die."

Keira completely ignored Ileana, keeping her gaze on Lance. "I rode that beast to get help. Unfortunately when I got to the road, I didn't quite clear the fence."

He stared at her in shock. "You rode the horse? By yourself?"

"I'm pretty sure it felt sorry for me. Well, until it saw the fence. Then it decided to get rid of me and veer the other way. The horse went left, I went straight. Before I could get my feet under me, some of Ileana's jerks grabbed me. So much for my attempt to save you."

"Enough!" Ileana yelled. "I'm about to vomit. Let's

get down to business. Our dearly departed Sam was nice enough to get cancer and decide he wanted to reunite with old friends before he died. That's what finally got the ball rolling again on the stupid OPI train and opened the door for me to find and eliminate the rest of you. I failed my uncle when things fell apart with that company. I finally have a chance to redeem myself now. All I need to do is find the last three team members. If you tell me nicely, I'll have both of you killed quickly. Continue to defy me and you'll suffer a slow, agonizing death. Your choice."

Keira finally turned and gave Ileana her full attention. "Don't you have to call your husband for permission to do any of this first?"

Ileana slapped her so fast Lance didn't get a chance to whip his legs out to stop her.

Keira ran her tongue over her freshly bleeding mouth, then smiled.

Lance was proud of her courage. But he wanted to shake her for angering Ileana further. He spoke again to distract Ileana from hurting Keira again.

"I don't know where they are," he said. "Who's this uncle you mentioned? Is he yours and your husband's mob contact? The one you both sold information to for years, causing innocent people to die?"

"Stop dragging Hudson into this. He's as moral and ethical as they come. And he never hit me by the way. This black eye was my doing, to get sympathy from Levi. Hudson would never hit a woman, even if she deserved it." She rolled her eyes, obviously not thinking of that as a compliment. "He never knew I was the one getting information. And the people who died were far from innocent. They were traitors, snitches, the worst of the worst. They deserved exactly what they got."

Lance made no attempt to hide his disgust. "How I ever thought you were a decent human being all those years ago is a mystery I'll likely never solve."

She screeched her rage again. But this time, she didn't stop to direct someone else. She hauled back to slap Lance just as she'd done to Keira. But this time he was ready for it. He whipped her legs out from under her and crashed down on top of her, twisting so the arm of the chair slammed against her throat. He was almost immediately yanked back up, still tied to the chair. But the damage was done. Ileana's face was already turning blue as she made gagging sounds and clawed at her crushed windpipe.

Her men all seemed to be in a state of panic, converging on her and dragging her into the dining room. They placed her on the table and started shouting orders at each other, trying to figure out how to help her.

Lance had been twisting and pulling at the ropes behind his back ever since he'd been captured. With the fall to the floor and him and his chair being hastily set back up, the ropes had loosened enough that he was able to yank his hands free.

Keira stared at him, her eyes wide with concern as he made short work of the rest of the ropes and knelt down behind her to work on hers.

"Go, go," she whispered. "Get out of here before they realize you're free."

"I'm not leaving you." He yanked and tugged at her ropes, swearing at how tight they were.

"I mean it, Lance. Please. I can't handle seeing you die. I'd rather die myself knowing you were going to be okay. Go."

He tugged at her ropes, finally loosening them. "I love

you too," he whispered, grinning as he yanked her up to standing.

"Hey, hey, stop!" one of the men yelled. He drew his gun.

Lance jumped in front of Keira, shielding her with his body.

"Wait," another man yelled at the first, shoving his hand up toward the ceiling just as the gun went off. "We can't kill them until she's done with them."

"Look at her," the shooter argued. "She's purple. She's not telling us anything."

Lance and Keira were already running for the front door, not waiting around as the argument continued behind them.

He threw the door open and they both ran outside. Lights flashed across their faces, making it impossible to see past them. The sound of dozens of guns being ratcheted and loaded had him glancing at Keira in frustration. "I'm so sorry."

She smiled. "Me too. I wanted to see how this thing between us ended. And I really wanted to find out what comes after the kissing part." She winked.

He grinned. Then they both raised their hands.

The sounds of men jogging toward them had Lance stepping in front of Keira again. She swore and tried to stand beside him. Just when they expected to be shot, the men passed them and ran inside the house.

Gunshots boomed. Glass shattered. Shouts and screams sounded.

"Get them out of here," a voice that Lance didn't recognize called out.

"We've got them."

That voice, he did recognize. He blinked against the harsh lights, then grinned when Trent and Asher ran up to them. Trent grabbed Lance's arm. Asher grabbed Keira.

They all raced off to the side of the house, away from the gunfire that was already slowing.

Kneeling down behind the engine block of one of the cars that had pulled up, the four of them waited until someone called for a cease-fire.

"All clear," someone from inside shouted.

People started running in and out of the house, taking control of the scene. Lance hugged Keira close to his side as they straightened. When yellow crime scene tape came out and someone began using it to cordon off the area, Lance and Keira looked at Trent and Asher in question.

"What's happening?" Lance asked. "Who are these people? How did you find us? What are—"

"Enough, enough." Trent grinned. "Ask Keira here. She's the one responsible for us getting here in the nick of time."

She blinked. "I am? What do you mean?"

"The text messages. We were already in the area because we'd hooked up with Hudson Vale to find Ileana and—"

"Wait," Lance said. "Ileana's husband? Isn't he the FBI mole?"

Asher shook his head, joining the conversation. "No. Ileana was the only mole. No one in the FBI was involved. She hacked OPI's computers and fed the info directly to a mob boss."

"Let me guess," Lance said. "Her uncle."

"Later you'll have to tell me how you knew that. Her relationship to him was buried under a web of changed names and forged birth certificates."

"It wasn't any brilliant investigative skills on my part," Lance said. "She told me a few minutes ago."

"Can we get back to these text messages you mentioned?" Keira said. "They blocked our cell phones. Nothing I sent could have gone through."

"They did," he said. "You must have gotten the phone out of the cell signal jammer range at some point, because the texts told us exactly where you were and what was going on. We—us and the FBI guys—were trying to figure out where exactly this farm was located. But until those texts came in, we were flying blind." He patted Keira on the shoulder. "You did it. You saved the day."

"No, I didn't. You all did." She smiled up at Lance. "And you did. You gave us both the time we needed to survive. You're my hero, truly."

He smiled and pressed a tender kiss against her forehead. "That's debatable. I'm just glad it all worked out. Or has it? Trent, Asher, you said you brought Vale here. Does that mean what I hope it means?"

They nodded. Trent said, "We have all the evidence we need to put Ileana away. And her uncle. Hudson Vale, the FBI, they had nothing to do with anything that happened. He was livid when he found out what Ileana had done. Due to a conflict of interest, of course, there's another FBI guy running this scene. But Hudson is here too. He wanted to be there when she was arrested."

"I don't think that's going to happen," Lance said.

"No? Why not?"

"I'm pretty sure she's dead."

They stared at him in surprise.

"I'm not proud of it," Lance said.

Keira tightened her arm around his waist. "There were at least a dozen armed men inside—"

"Ten," Lance corrected.

"Dozens more outside," Asher added.

"Right," Keira said. "In spite of all that, Lance did everything he could to protect me. And he did. Ileana would have killed us both. And even with all those thugs around us, and him tied to a chair, he managed to take her down. He truly saved both of us." She smiled. "But you two get credit too. You did arrive, as you said, in the nick of time."

They laughed, then sobered as a body bag was carried out the door, escorted in part by a very pale, defeated-looking man. Lance recognized him as Hudson Vale because of the research he'd done. From Keira's gasp beside him, he knew she did too. The man was moral and ethical, just as Ileana had accused. And in spite of what she'd done, which would no doubt end his career with the FBI, he'd ensured that justice was served.

An EMT ran up to Keira and Lance. "I was told you were both hurt. Do you need a stretcher?"

Keira looked up at Lance. "Your head is bleeding."

"It's mostly stopped now. You're black and blue. And your lip is bleeding."

"It's mostly stopped now."

They both laughed.

"We're fine," they told the EMT, laughing again when they said the same thing at the same time.

He gave them an odd look, then headed off in search of someone else to help.

"Hey, Lance. Catch."

He turned, and Trent tossed him something. A key fob. Lance looked at him in question.

"The only white SUV out here." He pointed. "Go on. You two have been through enough tonight. Head back to wherever you've been staying. Asher and I will catch a ride with someone else and we can talk tomorrow."

Keira frowned. "There aren't any hotels around here.

You can come to the house Lance rented. It's big enough for all of us."

Trent grinned. "I don't think Lance would agree with you. Like I said, we'll catch up tomorrow."

"Really late tomorrow," Lance called out.

Trent laughed as Lance grabbed Keira's hand and practically dragged her to the SUV. When they reached it, he turned her around so he could look in her eyes. He cupped her face with his hands and stared down at her in wonder. "I know it seems crazy to say this, so soon. But I've never been more sure of anything in my life. Keira, I—"

"—love you," they both said at the same time.

"Wow," she breathed.

"Wow," he echoed.

They kissed, and when they broke apart, tears were streaming down her cheeks.

"Keira? What's wrong?"

"They're happy tears. I suppose this means you'll be asking me for a date now."

He shook his head. "No. I've decided against that."

Her smiled faded. "What? I don't—"

"I was thinking of asking you something else instead. Marry me?"

She stared at him, her mouth falling open in shock.

The confidence he'd felt moments before took a dive. "Or, if it's too soon—"

She burst out laughing. "Too soon? We've never even been on a date."

"Right. Too soon. I've been worried this whole time about going too fast, about you possibly regretting this later. I want you to be sure, even though I know that I am. I'll wait as long as you want. We can take it slow and—"

"Yes!" She smiled. "The answer is yes!"

He stared at her, his mouth going dry. "Can you repeat that? I'm not sure that I heard you correctly. My ears are ringing."

"Which part? The yes that I'll marry you? Or the part where I tell you I am madly, deeply, forever in love with you? There will be no regrets, Lance. We can have a long engagement, if you need that to feel secure about me, about us. But I've never been so sure about anything. I love you. With everything that I am."

He groaned and kissed her again. This one was scorching hot. He pressed her against the SUV, fitting their bodies together. He kissed her the way he'd wanted to from the moment he'd seen how bravely she'd faced the gunmen at the cabin. She was an amazing woman in so many ways. Whether she wanted to return to Maple Falls and continue to be a cop or move to Gatlinburg with him and choose another career, they'd work it out. The only thing that mattered was being with her and living the rest of their lives together.

Whistles and catcalls had them breaking apart.

"Get a room," Asher called out.

Keira laughed. Lance rushed her around to the passenger side of the SUV and hurriedly fastened her seat belt. Then he was in the driver's seat racing them back toward their rental house.

When they arrived, he tenderly picked her up and carried her up the steps to the front door. Pausing in the opening, he held her in his arms and looked down at the most precious person he'd ever met. "I know we aren't married yet. And this isn't our home. But I still want to carry you over the threshold."

"That's so sweet. Since we're skipping a few steps, I'm

thinking we could skip another one. Let's start the honeymoon right now. That is, if you want to."

He cleared his suddenly raw throat, staring down at the beautiful woman in his arms. "How did I ever get so lucky to find you?"

"Hmm, I'm not sure. But you're definitely going to *get* lucky. If you hurry."

He eagerly ran inside carrying her, both of them laughing the whole time.

* * * * *

*If you missed the previous books
in Lena Diaz's miniseries,
A Tennessee Cold Case Story,
they're available now, wherever
Harlequin Intrigue books are sold!*

Murder on Prescott Mountain
Serial Slayer Cold Case
Shrouded in the Smokies
The Secret She Keeps
Smoky Mountains Graveyard